Leo Tolstoy

The fruits of culture

A comedy in four acts

Leo Tolstoy

The fruits of culture
A comedy in four acts

ISBN/EAN: 9783337104092

Printed in Europe, USA, Canada, Australia, Japan

Cover: Foto ©Andreas Hilbeck / pixelio.de

More available books at **www.hansebooks.com**

The Fruits of Culture

A COMEDY IN FOUR ACTS

BY N.

COUNT LEO TOLSTOI

TRANSLATED BY

GEORGE SCHUMM

––––––

BOSTON, MASS.
BENJ. R. TUCKER, PUBLISHER,
1891

THE FRUITS OF CULTURE.

THE CAST.

LEONID FEDOROVITCH SVESDINZEFF, a lieutenant of the Cavalry Guard a. D., proprietor of 24,000 desjatines in the various provinces. A vigorous man of about sixty, deferential, affable, gentlemanly. He is a believer in Spiritualism, and takes pleasure in startling people by the recital of his stories.

ANNA PAVLOVNA SVESDINZEFF, his wife, a stout, blooming lady, with the desire of appearing young. She entertains a strict regard for the conventional social forms, esteems her husband lightly, and puts a blind trust in her physician. An easily excitable lady.

BETSY, their daughter, a young lady of high society, about twenty years old. She is free in her manners, wears eyeglasses, flirts desperately, and laughs much. She talks very rapidly and very distinctly by moving her lips briskly like a foreigner.

VASSILI LEONIDITCH, their son, twenty-five years old, *Dr. juris*, without a practice, member of the Bicycle Club, the Race Club, and the Society for the Breeding of Greyhounds. A young man of excellent health and imperturbable self-possession. He talks loud and abruptly. Now perfectly serious, almost gloomy; now excessively gay, and laughing boisterously.

ALEXEI VLADIMIROVITCH KRUGOSVETLOFF, professor. A *savant*, about fifty years old, with quiet, deferential, and self-possessed manners in society, and a similar slow singing speech. He likes to hear himself talk. He maintains a contemptuous reserve towards those who do not agree with him. A great smoker. A lean, restless man.

THE PHYSICIAN, a healthy, corpulent man of about forty, with ruddy face. Noisy and blunt. With a self-complacent smile.

MARIA KONSTANTINOVNA, a girl of about twenty, a student at the Conservatory, with bangs, excessively modern dress, and of an insinuating and timid disposition.

PETRISTCHEFF, age twenty-eight, philologist, *Dr.*, on the look-out for a position, member of the same societies as Vassili Leoniditch, and, besides, of the Society for the Arrangement of Dances for Girls of the Common People, bald-headed. vivacious in movement and speech, very courteous.

THE BARONESS, a distinguished lady of about fifty; her movements are ponderous, and she talks in a monotone.

THE PRINCESS, a lady of the world, a guest.

THE PRINCESS'S DAUGHTER, a young lady of high society, a guest; she makes faces.

THE DUCHESS, an old-fashioned lady, who is hardly able to move about, with false locks and teeth.

GROSSMANN, of dark complexion and Jewish type, very lively, nervous; he talks very loud.

A Fat Lady, MARIA VASSILIEVNA TOLBUCHIN, a very distinguished, rich, and good-natured lady, acquainted with all the celebrities of the past and present. She is very fat, talks rapidly in order to silence the rest. She smokes.

BARON KLINGEN (Koko), Doctor of the University of St. Petersburg, chamberlain, an officer of the embassy. Perfectly correct, therefore of a tranquil mind and serenely happy.

A LADY.

A PROPRIETRESS (dumb person).

SACHATOFF, SERGEI IVANOVITCH, about fifty, Director of the Ministry a. D. An elegant gentleman of magnificent European culture. He is without employment, and takes an interest in all things. His carriage is dignified, indeed even somewhat reserved.

FEDOR IVANITCH, chamberlain, nearly sixty. An educated man, striving after culture. He uses his eyeglasses and his pocket-handkerchief, which he slowly unfolds too liberally. He also takes an interest in politics. A sensible and good man.

GREGORI, lackey, twenty-eight years, a handsome fellow, but dissolute, envious, and insolent.

JACOB, forty years, butler, a restless, good-natured man, who concerns himself only about the family affairs of the peasants.

SEMION, kitchen boy. A healthy, fresh-looking peasant boy, blonde, still beardless, quiet, with a friendly smile.

THE COACHMAN, thirty-five years. A fop, he lets only his moustache grow; rude and positive.

THE OLD COOK, forty-five years, with bristly hair, unshaven, bloated yellowish face, and trembling hands, in a ragged Nanking spring overcoat, dirty pantaloons, and torn shoes; he is hoarse. He utters his words as if he had first to overcome an obstacle.

THE COOK, a gossip; she is discontented, about thirty years old.

THE STEWARD, a retired soldier.

TANIA, chambermaid, nineteen years old, an energetic, strong, jolly girl, with quickly changing moods. In moments of powerful joyous excitement, she squeals.

FIRST PEASANT, sixty years, formerly alderman of the town; thinks he knows how to associate with gentlemen, and likes to hear himself talk.

SECOND PEASANT, forty-five years, proprietor, rude and downright, a man of few words. Semion's father.

THIRD PEASANT, seventy years, in bast shoes, nervous, restless, always in a hurry, shy; he tries to drown his shyness by words.

FIRST FOOTMAN of the Duchess. An old man of the old type, with the vanity of his class.

SECOND FOOTMAN, a healthy, coarse giant.

A PARCEL CARRIER. In blue jacket, with clean, ruddy face. He talks with decision, impressively and distinctly.

The action takes place at the capital in the house of the Svesdinzeffs.

ACT I.

The stage represents the hall of a wealthy house in Moscow. Three doors: the outer door, the door of LEONID FEDOROVITCH'S *study, and the door of* VASSILI LEONIDITCH'S *room. A stairway leads to the sitting rooms; back of the stairs a passage to the buffet.*

SCENE I.

GREGORI (*a young, handsome lackey; views himself in the glass and makes himself fine*).

Gregori. Too bad about that moustache. A lackey, their highnesses say, must not have a moustache. And why? That everybody may know you are a lackey. One might easily cut out their darling son. Hm, bah! even without a moustache I can challenge him. (*Views himself smiling in the glass.*) And how many girls run after me! But I like none so well as this Tania. Only a chambermaid! Well — yes! But still, prettier than the gracious young lady. (*Smiles.*) And comely she is! (*Listens.*) I hear her coming! (*Smiles.*) And how she clatters with her heels ... Ha!

SCENE II.

GREGORI *and* TANIA *with a fur jacket and bootlets.*

Gregori. Your humble servant, Miss Tatiana!

Tania. What, always before the glass? You surely think you are very handsome?

Gregori. Am I then not good-looking?

Tania. So so, neither handsome nor ugly, something between the two. What's the meaning of all these furs hanging about here?

Gregori. I shall instantly remove them, Miss. (*He takes down a fur, puts it on Tania, and embraces her.*) Tania, what I was going to say to you . . .

Tania. Get you gone with your saying! Is this proper? (*She tears herself angrily away.*) I say, let me alone!

Gregori (*looking around*). Do give me a kiss!

Tania. What are you thinking, anyway? I will give you such a kiss. . . . (*She lifts her arm to strike.*)

Vassili Leoniditch. (*A bell rings behind the scene, then he calls.*) Gregori!

Tania. You see! Go in there, your master calls!

Gregori. He can wait; he has but just opened his eyes. Tell me, why do you not love me?

Tania. What are you talking about loving? I love nobody!

Gregori. Not so! You love Semka! He is of the right sort, a kitchen boy with red paws!

Tania. Be he what he may, yet you are jealous of him!

Vassili Leoniditch (behind the scene). Gregori!!

Gregori. You can wait! ... It's worth while to be jealous of him! Is it for that you've got your culture, to set your cap for him? If you loved me, that would be something ... Tania ...

Tania (angry and severe). I say it is all in vain.

Vassili Leoniditch (behind the scene). Gregori!!!

Gregori. You are awfully severe.

Vassili Leoniditch (behind the scene, calling persistently, monotonously, and with all his might). Gregori, Gregori, Gregori!

(TANIA *and* GREGORI *laugh.*)

Gregori. If you knew what sort of girls have been sweet on me!

(*The bell rings.*)

Tania. Go to your master now, and let me alone.

Gregori. I see you are stupid. Of course, I am not Semion.

Tania. Semion thinks of marrying, and not of fooling.

Scene III.

GREGORI, TANIA, *and* PARCEL CARRIER (*carries a large box with a dress*).

Carrier. Good morning!
Gregori. Good morning! From whom?
Carrier. From Bourdé the dress, and here is a letter for the lady.
Tania (takes the letter). Sit down, I will deliver it. (*Exit.*)

Scene IV.

GREGORI, CARRIER, *and* VASSILI LEONIDITCH (*appears in shirt-sleeves and slippers at the door*).

Vassili Leoniditch. Gregori!
Gregori. Command me, Sir!
Vassili Leoniditch. Gregori, are you deaf?

Gregori. I have just come.

Vassili Leoniditch. Warm water and tea!

Gregori. Semion will bring it immediately.

Vassili Leoniditch. And what's that? From Bourdiet?

(*Exeunt* VASSILI LEONIDITCH *and* GREGORI. *The bell rings.*)

Carrier. Your servant, Sir!

SCENE V.

CARRIER *and* TANIA (*enters and opens the door*).

Tania (*to the Carrier*). Wait!

Carrier. I am waiting.

SCENE VI.

CARRIER, TANIA, *and* SACHATOFF (*enters*).

Tania. Pardon me, Sir, the lackey went away this moment. But please to come nearer. Permit me. (*Takes off his fur.*)

Sachatoff (*arranging his dress*). Is Leonid Fedorovitch at home? Already up?

(*The bell rings.*)

Tania. Certainly. Long ago!

Scene VII.

The Same.   The Physician *(enters).*

Physician (looking around for the lackey.   He observes Sachatoff, deferentially).   Ah, I have the honor ?

Sachatoff (looking sharply).   The doctor, if I mistake not ?

Physician.   And I had thought you were abroad.   Did you come to see Leonid Fedorovitch ?

Sachatoff.   Yes.   And you ?   Is somebody ill perhaps ?

Physician (smiling).   Well, not exactly ill, but you know what trouble we have with the ladies !   Till three o'clock each day she sits at the card table, and off and on indulges in a glass, too.   And withal she is fat and stout, and carries a few years on her back moreover.

Sachatoff.   Do you give Anna Pavlovna also your diagnosis so plainly ?   I imagine that would hardly please her.

Physician (laughing).   What, am I not right ? They indulge themselves in all sorts of ways, impaired digestion follows, pressure on the liver, nervous troubles,—the whole train of ills; then we are to mend the mischief. They give us no end of trouble! (*He smiles.*) And you, are you not also a Spiritualist?

Sachatoff. I? No, I am not also a Spiritualist.... Well, good bye! (*He wants to go; the physician holds him back.*)

Physician. No, no, I don't entirely deny Spiritualism either; if a man like Krugosvetloff espouses the cause. How were it possible, too? A professor, of European fame. Surely there must be something in it. I should like to attend one of their *séances.* But I cannot well afford the time, one is so busy.

Sachatoff. Yes, I readily believe you.— Good bye! (*Exit with a slight salute.*)

Physician (*to Tania*). Up already?

Tania. They are in the bedroom. Please, just enter.

(SACHATOFF *and the* PHYSICIAN *leave by different doors.*)

Scene VIII.

CARRIER, TANIA, *and* FEDOR IVANITCH (*enters holding a newspaper*).

Fedor Ivanitch (*to the Carrier*). What do you want?

Carrier. The dress from Bourdé and a letter. I was told to wait.

Fedor Ivanitch. Ah, from Bourdiet! (*To Tania.*) Who has just been here?

Tania. Sachatoff and the doctor. They stood here a little while and talked, only about Spirituism.

Fedor Ivanitch (*correcting*). About Spiritualism.

Tania. I said so, about Spirituism. Have you already heard, Fedor Ivanitch, how well everything went off last time? (*She laughs.*) There were rappings, and things flew through the air.

Fedor Ivanitch. How do you know that?

Tania. The young lady said so.

Scene IX.

TANIA, FEDOR IVANITCH, CARRIER, *and* JACOB, *the butler* (*rushing in with a glass of tea*).

Jacob (*to the Carrier*). How do you do?
Carrier (*gloomy*). How do you do?

(JACOB *knocks at* VASSILI LEONIDITCH'S *door.*)

Scene X.

The Same and Gregori.

Gregori. Let me have it.

Jacob. The glasses of yesterday have not yet been returned, nor the tray from Vassili Leoniditch's. But I am held responsible.

Gregori. The tray is in his room, full of cigarettes.

Jacob. Then put them somewhere else. For I am asked for it.

Gregori. I'll fetch it, I'll fetch it !

Jacob. I'll fetch it,— yes, where is it? Just when one needs it most it is not here.

Gregori. But, I tell you, I'll fetch it. Don't make such a fuss !

Jacob. It's easy for you to talk, but I — for the third time I am ordered to serve tea, prepare breakfast. Forever up and down, that's the way it goes from day to day. Who works harder than I in this house? And always there is fault to be found.

Gregori. Where is there a more efficient person? Indeed, very efficient.

Tania. In your eyes there is but one who is efficient, you . . .

Gregori (to Tania). You have not been asked! (*Exit.*)

SCENE XI.

TANIA, JACOB, FEDOR IVANITCH, *and the* CARRIER.

Jacob. Well, it's all right, I don't feel hurt. Miss Tatiana, didn't her ladyship have any-thing at all to say about yesterday?

Tania. About the lamp?

Jacob. How was it possible that it could fall out of my hand! God knows. I was just going to wipe it, barely touched it — bang, there it lay. All in small pieces. I am always unlucky! It's easy for Gregori Michailitch to talk, he is single, but when one has a family one must keep his senses together, if he wants to be fed. I am not afraid of work. So she hasn't said a word? Thank God! How many tea-spoons have you, Fedor Ivanitch, one or two?

Fedor Ivanitch. One, one. (*Reading the newspaper.*)

(*Exit* JACOB.)

SCENE XII.

TANIA, FEDOR IVANITCH, *and the* CARRIER. *A bell rings.* GREGORI, *with a tray, and the* STEWARD *enter.*

Steward (to Gregori). Tell his lordship, peasants from the village are here.

Gregori (pointing to Fedor Ivanitch). Tell the chamberlain, I have no time. (*Exit.*)

SCENE XIII.

TANIA, FEDOR IVANITCH, STEWARD, *and the* CARRIER.

Tania. Where do the peasants come from?

Steward. From the neighborhood of Kursk, I think.

Tania (squeals). It's they . . . That is Semion's father, on account of the land. I shall go meet them. (*Runs away.*)

SCENE XIV.

FEDOR IVANITCH, *the* STEWARD, *and the* CARRIER.

Steward. What's to be done? Shall I admit them, or what? They say — on account of the land, his lordship knows.

Fedor Ivanitch. Yes, on account of the purchase of the land. That is so. There is a visitor with him now. Go say they must wait.

Steward. But where shall they wait?

Fedor Ivanitch. They are to wait in the court, I will have them called.

(*Exit* STEWARD.)

SCENE XV

FEDOR IVANITCH, TANIA, *three peasants following her,* GREGORI, *and the* CARRIER.

Tania. To the right. Here, here!

Fedor Ivanitch. Did I not tell you not to bring them here?

Gregori. Yes, yes, she is like quicksilver.

Tania. Never mind, Fedor Ivanitch, they will stand here in the corner.

Fedor Ivanitch. They will soil everything.

Tania. They have scraped their feet, and I will scrub again. (*To the peasants.*) Stand here.

(*The peasants enter, carrying bundles of wheat-bread, eggs, and towels for presents. They are looking for the crucifix in the corner. They cross themselves in the direction of the stairs; bow before* FEDOR IVANITCH, *and stand up stiffly against the wall.*)

Gregori (to Fedor Ivanitch). Fedor Ivanitch! People say only Pironné can make bootlets; just look at this one's boots! (*He points to the third peasant in bast shoes.*)

Fedor Ivanitch. You must always poke fun at people.

(*Exit* GREGORI.)

SCENE XVI.

TANIA, FEDOR IVANITCH, *and the three peasants.*

Fedor Ivanitch (rises and approaches the peasants). So you are from Kursk? You have come to see about that land purchase?

First Peasant. So it is, Sir! That is, so to speak, we are here to complete the purchase of the land. If his lordship could be told of this?

Fedor Ivanitch. Yes, yes, I understand, I understand. Wait here, and I will at once let him know. (*Exit.*)

SCENE XVII.

TANIA *and the three peasants,* VASSILI LEONIDITCH (*behind the scene*). *The peasants look around; they are embarrassed, uncertain what to do with the presents.*

First Peasant. What do you call it . . . that . . . I don't know what they call it . . . on which to put this, properly, so that it looks like something. A plate or what?

Tania. Let me see, let me see. Just hand it over, meanwhile it may lie here. (*She puts the things on the settee.*)

First Peasant. What position, so to speak, does the gentleman occupy who spoke to us?

Tania. He is the chamberlain.

First Peasant. Simply, chamberman. That means something like always around his lordship. (*To Tania.*) And you, so to speak, are you also of the service?

Tania. I am the chambermaid. I too am from Demba. And I know you, and you, too, only this countryman I don't know. (*She points to the third peasant.*)

Third Peasant. These you have recognized, and me you do not recognize?

Tania. Are you Jefim Antonitch?

First Peasant. Real-ly!

Tania. And you are Semion's father, Sachar Trifonitch?

Second Peasant. Correct!

Third Peasant. And I, say I, Mitri Tchilikin. Do you know me now?

Tania. Now I know you also.

Second Peasant. And to whom do you belong?

Tania. I am the daughter of Aksinia, the soldier's wife, an orphan.

First and Third Peasants. 'm, 'm ?!

Second Peasant. It's not without reason they say: Go buy thee some swine, then dress them up fine, in silk how they'll shine.

First Peasant. Real-ly. Just so, precisely like a young lady.

Third Peasant. How that comes. Great God!

Vassili Leoniditch (behind the scene. He rings the bell, then calls). Gregori! Gregori!

First Peasant. Who is getting so excited there, so to speak?

Tania. That's the young gentleman.

Third Peasant. Gracious God! I said at first, better wait outdoors until our turn comes. (*Pause.*)

Second Peasant. So it is you Semion wants to take for wife?

Tania. Did he write? (*Hides behind her apron.*)

Second Peasant. Of course he wrote! He is not in his senses! The boy, I see, has become a fine gentleman.

Tania (lively). He has not become a fine gentleman at all. Shall I send him here?

Second Peasant.   Why send him here?
There's no hurry.   We shall see each other yet!

(VASSILI LEONIDITCH *is heard calling in despair:
"Gregori! The devil take you!"*)

SCENE XVIII.

The Same.   (VASSILI LEONIDITCH *comes through the
door in his shirt-sleeves.   He adjusts his eyeglasses.*)

Vassili Leoniditch.   Is the house deserted?
Tania.   He is not here, Vassili Leoniditch.
I'll have him called at once.   (*Goes towards the
door.*)
Vassili Leoniditch.   I hear talking.   What
sort of scarecrows are these?   What?   Eh?
Tania.   These are peasant people from a
village in Kursk, Vassili Leoniditch.
Vassili Leoniditch (*pointing to the Carrier*).
And that one?   Ah, yes, from Bourdiet.   (*The
peasants bow.*)

(VASSILI LEONIDITCH *pays no attention to them.*   GRE-
GORI *comes towards* TANIA *at the door.*   TANIA *remains.*)

SCENE XIX.

The Same and GREGORI.

Vassili Leoniditch.   Did I not tell you the
other shoes?   I cannot wear these!   ·

Gregori. The others are there also.

Vassili Leoniditch. Where is there?

Gregori. Well, also there.

Vassili Leoniditch. You lie!

Gregori. You will see.

(*Exeunt* VASSILI LEONIDITCH *and* GREGORI.)

SCENE XX.

TANIA, *the three peasants, and the* CARRIER.

Third Peasant. And maybe, I say, this is not the right time, then we can go to our lodgings and wait there.

Tania. No, just wait. I will get you some plates for your presents. (*Exit.*)

SCENE XXI.

The Same. SACHATOFF, LEONID FEDOROVITCH, *followed by* FEDOR IVANITCH.

(*The peasants take up their presents and get into position.*)

Leonid Fedorovitch (to the peasants). In a minute, in a minute, just wait — (*Pointing to the Carrier.*) Who is that?

Carrier: From Bourdé.

Leonid Fedorovitch. Ah, from Bourdiet!

Sachatoff (*smiling*).   I don't exactly deny it ;
but you will admit that those of us who have not
witnessed all this you are telling about, and
uninitiated as we are, can hardly believe it.

Leonid Fedorovitch.   You say : I cannot believe it.   But neither do we demand faith.   We
demand examination.   Is it possible that I
should not believe in this ring?   And I got
this ring from there.

· *Sachatoff.*   Where is from there ?   Where,
where ?

Leonid Fedorovitch.   From   the   beyond.
Yes.

Sachatoff (*smiling*).   Exceedingly interesting,
exceedingly interesting !

Leonid Fedorovitch.   Well, then, you think I
am too enthusiastic, that I see by imagination
what is not ; but Alexei Vladimirovitch Krugosvetloff ! .He surely is no second-rate man,
he is a professor — and he also admits it.   And
he does not stand alone either.   Crookes and
Wallace ?

Sachatoff.   Indeed, I do not deny.   I only
say it is exceedingly interesting.   I should like
to know, too, how Krugosvetloff explains it.

Leonid Fedorovitch.   He has his own theory!
But do come and see us this evening ; he will

surely be here. First Grossmann . . . You know, the celebrated mind-reader.

Sachatoff. Yes, I have heard of him ; but I have never seen him.

Leonid Fedorovitch. Come then. First Grossmann, then Kaptchitch, and our medium-istic *séance.* . . . (*To Fedor Ivanitch.*) Has the messenger not yet returned from Kaptchitch ?

Fedor Ivanitch. He is not yet back.

Sachatoff. How am I to know then ?

Leonid Fedorovitch. Just come, in any case come. Even if Kaptchitch should not be present, we will get our medium. Maria Ignatievna is a medium ; to be sure, not such a good one as Kaptchitch, but nevertheless . . .

Scene XXII.

The Same and Tania. (*She goes to the presents with the plates and listens to the conversation.*)

Sachatoff (*smiling*). Yes, yes. But tell me one thing : how is it that the mediums invariably belong to the so-called cultured sphere ? Kaptchitch, Maria Ignatievna. If this is a special force, we ought to meet it also among the common people, among the peasants.

Leonid Fedorovitch. Such is the case, too.

It is very often the case. We have *one* peasant in the house, and he is a medium. We called him recently during the *séance*. The sofa was to be moved, and we had no thought of him. And he probably must have fallen asleep. Now imagine. Our *séance* was already approaching its end ; Kaptchitch awoke. Suddenly we observe in the other corner of the room, where the peasant is sitting, mediumistic phenomena : the table moves from the spot and begins to walk.

Tania (aside). That was when I crept from under the table.

Leonid Fedorovitch. Plainly he is also a medium. The more so as he very much resembles Home. Do you remember Home ? the blonde man with the innocent face ?

Sachatoff (shrugging his shoulders). Indeed, that is very interesting. Of course you must make your experiments with him.

Leonid Fedorovitch. We are going to do that, too. And he is not the only one. There are mediums without number. Only we don't know them. It is but a few days since an invalid old lady moved a wall from the spot.

Sachatoff. Moved a wall from the spot ?

Leonid Fedorovitch. Yes, yes. She was

lying in bed, and had no idea that she was a medium. She propped herself with her hand against the wall, and the wall moved from the spot.

Sachatoff. And did not cave in?

Leonid Fedorovitch. And did not cave in.

Sachatoff. Strange! Very well, I will come in the evening!

Leonid Fedorovitch. Just come, just come, the *séance* will take place in any case.

(SACHATOFF *gets ready*, LEONID FEDOROVITCH *accompanies him to the door*.)

SCENE XXIII.

The Same except SACHATOFF.

Carrier (*to Tania*). Will you not announce me to her ladyship? I surely can't stay here over night!

Tania. Wait. Her ladyship and the young lady intend taking a drive; they must pass this way. (*Exit.*)

SCENE XXIV.

The Same except TANIA.

Leonid Fedorovitch (*approaches the peasants; they bow before him and offer their presents*). That is not necessary!

First Peasant (*smiling*). It is our first duty. Besides, the commune told us to.

Second Peasant. It is customary so.

Third Peasant. It's not worth while to waste many words... We are very contented... As our fathers, I say, served your fathers, I say, so also we wish from the bottom of our heart, not that we would ... (*He bows.*)

Leonid Fedorovitch. What now? What do you want?

First Peasant. We want to see your lordship.

Scene XXV.

The Same and Petristcheff (*enters quickly, in a gray cloak*).

Petristcheff. Is Vassili Leoniditch up yet? (*He sees Leonid Fedorovitch, and salutes him with a nod of the head.*)

Leonid Fedorovitch. You wish to speak with my son?

Petristcheff. I? Yes, I wished to see Wowó a minute!

Leonid Fedorovitch. Please to pass along.

(Petristcheff *takes off his cloak, and walks quickly away.*)

Scene XXVI.

The Same except PETRISTCHEFF.

Leonid Fedorovitch (*to the peasants*).   Well, now.   What do you want?

Second Peasant.   Please accept our presents.

First Peasant (*smiling*).   That is, the gifts from the village.

Third Peasant.   And without wasting words — it's not worth while.   We wish you every-thing that is good, as to a father.   And without wasting words!

Leonid Fedorovitch.   Very well. . . . Fedor, take them!

Fedor Ivanitch.   All right, let me have them (*takes the presents*).

Leonid Fedorovitch.   What business brings you here?

First Peasant.   We come to your lordship.

Leonid Fedorovitch.   I see that you come to me; but what do you want?

First Peasant.   To complete the purchase. The question is . . .

Leonid Fedorovitch.   How, do you want to purchase the land, or what?

First Peasant.   Real-ly, so it is.   The question is . . . that is, to acquire the land as our property. And the commune has empowered us, so to speak, to go to the imperial bank, as is customary, and get a stamp at the prescribed price.

Leonid Fedorovitch. That is, you want to buy the land through the mediation of the bank, is that not so, or how?

First Peasant. So it is, as you proposed to us in the summer. The whole sum that must be got together, if the land is to become our property, amounts to 32,864 roubles.

Leonid Fedorovitch. Very well, but how about the payment?

First Peasant. And the payment, as was agreed in the summer, the commune proposes to divide into installments and cash down, as is written in the law, 4000 roubles on a table.

Second Peasant. That is, the 4000 roubles cash now, and the rest later.

Third Peasant (producing the money meanwhile). You can believe we pledge ourselves personally, and it will surely not be that . . . and, I say, so or so, or this, I say . . . all that is right.

Leonid Fedorovitch. But I wrote you that I would agree only on condition that you get the whole sum together.

First Peasant. Yes, real-ly, that would surely be better ; but, that is, it is impossible.

Leonid Fedorovitch. What's to be done, then ?

First Peasant. The commune had hoped, so to speak, as you proposed in the summer, to pay by installments . . .

Leonid Fedorovitch. That was last year; then I agreed to it, but now I cannot . . .

Second Peasant. But that won't do. You gave us hope, we prepared the document, and got the money together.

Third Peasant. Have mercy, Sir! Our land is small, hardly a hen — not to say any-thing of cattle — hardly a hen, I say, has room. (*He bows.*) Do not transgress, Sir. (*Bows.*)

Leonid Fedorovitch. It is true I agreed to payment by installments last year, but circum-stances . . . so that I cannot well do it now.

Second Peasant. We need the land to sup-port life.

First Peasant. Real-ly, without the land our life is forfeited and doomed.

Third Peasant (bows). Sir! The land is small, hardly a hen — not to say anything of cattle — hardly a hen, I say, has room! Sir, have mercy! Take the money, Sir!

Leonid Fedorovitch (has looked at the paper meanwhile). I understand you, I should my-self gladly help you. Wait here. I will give you an answer in half an hour. Fedor, see that no one is admitted.

Fedor Ivanitch. Very well, your lordship.

(*Exit* LEONID FEDOROVITCH.)

SCENE XXVII.

The Same except LEONID FEDOROVITCH. (*The peasants are depressed.*)

Second Peasant. A fine affair! To give the whole, he says. Yes, where get it?

First Peasant. If he had not given us hope in the summer. So we believed, real-ly, it would be as we had agreed in the summer.

Third Peasant. Gracious God! And I have already taken out the money. (*He rolls the money up again.*) What are we to do now?

Fedor Ivanitch. What is the business that brought you here?

First Peasant. Our business, dear sir, is, so to speak, somewhat like this : He proposed to us in the summer to pay by installments; the commune agreed to this, and gave us power to act; and now he proposes, so to speak, that we

pay the whole sum cash down. Well, now, that
is quite impossible.

Fedor Ivanitch. How much money have
you?

First Peasant. For the first payment 4000
roubles, that is, all in all.

Fedor Ivanitch. Well? Make an effort, get
more together.

First Peasant. We have already been from
house to house. The people have no brains in
their head, Sir.

Second Peasant. Where there is nothing,
the emperor has lost his right.

Third Peasant. We should indeed like to,
with our whole heart. But we have already had
to get this together by force.

Scene XXVIII.

The Same, Vassili Leoniditch, *and* Petristcheff
(in the door, both with cigarettes).

Vassili Leoniditch. I have already said that
I will try. I will try as far as lies in my power.
Well?

Petristcheff. Only consider, if you do not
get it, the devil knows how badly it may go
with us!

Vassili Leoniditch. I have said once I will try, and then it will be done, too. Eh?

Petristcheff. Very well. I only say you must get it at all hazards. I will wait. (*Exit, closing the door behind him.*)

Scene XXIX.

The Same except PETRISTCHEFF.

Vassili Leoniditch (*with a movement of the hand*). The devil knows what that is.

(*The peasants bow.*)

Vassili Leoniditch (*seeing the Carrier, to Fedor Ivanitch*). Why do you not dismiss the man from Bourdiet? Or perhaps he has taken his lodgings with us altogether? Just see, he has fallen asleep. Eh?

Fedor Ivanitch. The letter is already delivered. He was told to wait until Anna Pavlovna comes.

Vassili Leoniditch (*looks over to the peasants, and views the money with covetous eyes*) Ah! what's that? Money? For whom? Money for us? (*To Fedor Ivanitch.*) Who are these people?

Fedor Ivanitch. They are countrymen from the neighborhood of Kursk; they want to buy land.

Vassili Leoniditch. Well, how is it, is the sale already completed?

Fedor Ivanitch. No, there is no agreement yet. They are very miserly.

Vassili Leoniditch. So? We must talk to them. (*To the peasants.*) Well, will you purchase, eh?

First Peasant. Real-ly, we propose that it shall be so that we possess land as our property.

Vassili Leoniditch. Then you must not be so miserly. Listen, you know how much the peasant needs land! Eh? Very much.

First Peasant. Real-ly, land is the most important thing to the peasant. That is true.

Vassili Leoniditch. You must not be miserly then. For what does land signify? On the land you can sow wheat in beds, you see. You can get 300 poods, the pood a rouble, 300 roubles, eh? . . . And, then, just think of mint, I tell you you can make a thousand roubles to a desjatine.

First Peasant. Real-ly, quite truly, one can raise all products when one knows how.

Vassili Leoniditch. Mint, then, mint. For I have studied that, that is printed in the books. I will show you. Eh?

First Peasant. Real-ly, all that is to be learned better out of books. Culture is every-thing.

Vassili Leoniditch. Purchase then, don't be miserly, and give the money. (*To Fedor Ivanitch*). Where is papa?

Fedor Ivanitch. In his room. He wished not to be disturbed now.

.*Vassili Leoniditch.* What, he is surely ask-ing the spirits whether he shall sell the land or not? Eh?

Fedor Ivanitch. I cannot say. I know that he went away undecided.

Vassili Leoniditch. What do you think, Fedor Ivanitch, has he money? Eh?

Fedor Ivanitch. I do not know. Hardly. Why do you wish to know that? Did you not get a nice check last week?

Vassili Leoniditch. I spent that for the dogs. And now, you know, our new club, Petristcheff is elected, and I had some money from Petristcheff, and now I must pay the initi-ation fee for him and for myself. Eh?

Fedor Ivanitch. Of which new club are you speaking? Of the Bicycle Club?

Vassili Leoniditch. No, I will tell you pres-ently: an entirely new club. A very serious club, I tell you. And do you know who the chairman is? Eh?

Fedor Ivanitch. But what kind of a new club?

Vassili Leoniditch. A club for the breeding of old Russian shock dogs. Eh? And I tell you: to-night is our first meeting and banquet. And I have no money! I want to see him! I will try! (*Exit through the door.*)

Scene XXX.

The peasants, Fedor Ivanitch, *and the* Carrier.

First Peasant (to Fedor Ivanitch). Who is that, Sir?

Fedor Ivanitch (smiling). The young gentleman.

Third Peasant. The son of the house, so to speak. Gracious God! (*He puts away the money.*) One must put it away while it is yet time, I see.

First Peasant. And we have been told that he serves in the military, in the cavalry, so to speak.

Fedor Ivanitch. No, as the only son he is exempt from military service.

Third Peasant. Suffered to stay home, let

us say, for the support of his parents.   That
is right.

Second Peasant (nodding with his head).
And he will support them, there's not a word
to waste over that.

Third Peasant.   Gracious God!

Scene XXXI.

Fedor Ivanitch, *the three peasants,* Vassili Leoniditch, *followed by* Leonid Fedorovitch, *who remains at the door.*

Vassili Leoniditch.   It is always so.   Truly
remarkable.   First they say, why have you no
employment — and then, when I have found a
field of activity and am at work — if a serious
club is founded for a noble purpose, then 300
beggarly roubles cannot be spared! . . .

Leonid Fedorovitch.   When I say I cannot, I
cannot.   I haven't got it.

Vassili Leoniditch.   But you have sold land.

Leonid Fedorovitch.   In the first place, I
haven't sold anything, and above all, — leave
me in peace.   You have already heard that I
haven't any time.   (*Slams the door.*)

Scene XXXII.

The Same except Leonid Fedorovitch.

Fedor Ivanitch. I told you at first this was not the right time.

Vassili Leoniditch. A nice scrape to get into, eh? I'll go to mamma; she is my last hope. That's what I call going mad on Spiritualism, and forgetting all else. (*He goes upstairs.*)

(Fedor Ivanitch *sits down and takes up a newspaper*).

Scene XXXIII.

The Same, Betsy *and* Maria Konstantinovna *come downstairs;* Gregori *follows them.*

Betsy. Is the carriage ready?

Gregori. It is just driving up.

Betsy (to Maria Konstantinovna). Let us go, let us go. I saw it was he.

Maria Konstantinovna. Which he?

Betsy. You know very well — Petristcheff.

Maria Konstantinovna. But where is he then?

Betsy. He is with Wowó; you will soon see.

Maria Konstantinovna.　And if it is not he?

(*The peasants and the Carrier bow.*)

Betsy (*to the Carrier*).　Ah, you are from Bourdiet with the dress.

Carrier.　Yes, gracious miss.　May it please you to attend to this matter.

Betsy.　I know nothing about it.　That is mamma's affair.

Carrier.　I am not expected to know that. I have orders to deliver the goods and receive the money.

Betsy.　Wait, then.

Maria Konstantinovna.　Is it the costume for the charade again?

Betsy.　Yes, a charming costume.　And mamma will not take it and will not pay for it.

Maria Konstantinovna.　And why?

Betsy.　You must ask mamma about that. To give Wowó 500 roubles for dogs, that is not too much; and 100 roubles for a dress is too much.　I surely can't appear as a scarecrow. (*Pointing to the peasants.*)　And who are these people?

Gregori.　Peasants; land, I believe, they want to buy.

Betsy.　I thought hunters; are they not hunters?

First Peasant. Surely not, lady, we have come to Leonid Fedorovitch for the purpose of completing the act of the purchase of the land.

Betsy. How is it, hunters were to have come to Wowó? And are you surely not hunters? (*The peasants are silent.*) How stupid they are! (*She goes to the door.*) Wowó! (*Laughs.*)

Maria Konstantinovna. You have just met him.

Betsy. That was a clever stroke! ... Wowó, are you in there?

SCENE XXXIV.

The Same and PETRISTCHEFF.

Petristcheff. Wowó is not here; but I am willing, in his stead, to do all that is desired. I salute you! I salute you, Maria Konstantinovna! (*He first shakes Betsy's hand long and vigorously, then Maria Konstantinovna's.*)

Second Peasant. Just see, as if he were pumping water.

Betsy. You cannot represent him, but at any rate it's better than nothing. (*She laughs.*) What's the business you have with Wowó?

Petristcheff. Business? Fi—nancial business, that is, our business is fi! and at the same time nancial business, and besides financial business.

Betsy. What is the meaning of nancial business, anyway?

Petristcheff. A fine question! That's the joke of it, that it means nothing.

Betsy. Well, that I call missing the mark, missing it awfully. (*They laugh.*)

Petristcheff. It is impossible for one always to hit the bull's eye. That is a kind of lottery. A blank, and again a blank, and for once, perhaps, the capital prize.

(*Exit* FEDOR IVANITCH *into* LEONID FEDOROVITCH'S *study.*)

SCENE XXXV.

The Same except FEDOR IVANITCH.

Betsy. That was missing the mark. Tell me, were you at Mergassoff's yesterday?

Petristcheff. Not at *Mère* Gassoff's, rather at *Père* Gassoff's, and not at *Père* Gassoff's, either, but at *Fils* Gassoff's.

Betsy. Is it utterly impossible for you to suppress these *jeu de mots*? That is an inveterate vice.—Were there gypsies there also? (*She laughs.*)

Petristcheff (*sings*). "*Auf den Schürzen Hähnelein — Mit den goldenen Kämmelein*" —

Betsy. Happy people ! And we were bored at Fofó's.

Petristcheff (*continues singing*). "*Und versprach ihr süsses Mündchen — Mir*" . . . How does it go ? Maria Konstantinovna, how does it go ?

Maria Konstantinovna. "*Mir ein holdes Schäferstündchen*" . . .

Petristcheff. What ? What ? Maria Konstantinovna ? (*He laughs.*)

Betsy. *Cessez, vous devenez impossible !*

Petristcheff. *J'ai cessé, j'ai bébé, j'ai dédé* . . .

Betsy. I see but one means of escaping your jests — I must let you sing. Come with me to Wowó's room ; he has a guitar, too. Come, Maria Konstantinovna, come !

(BETSY, MARIA KONSTANTINOVNA, *and* PETRISTCHEFF *go away into* VASSILI LEONIDITCH'S *room.*)

SCENE XXXVI.

GREGORI, *the three peasants, and the* CARRIER.

First Peasant. To whom do these belong ?

Gregori. The one — is the young miss ; the other — the music teacher ; she gives music lessons.

First Peasant. She occupies herself, so to speak, with study. And how accurate she is! As if painted.

Second Peasant. Why don't they marry? She is surely of the right age.

Gregori. You think, as among you, that the right age is fifteen years?

First Peasant. And the young fellow there is, so to speak, a musician?

Gregori (mocking him). Musician! ... You know simply nothing.

First Peasant. Real-ly true, that is our ignorance, our want of culture, so to speak.

Third Peasant. Gracious God!

(*Gypsy songs accompanied by the guitar are heard in* VASSILI LEONIDITCH'S *room.*)

SCENE XXXVII.

GREGORI, *the three peasants, the* CARRIER. SEMION *enters; he is followed by* TANIA. TANIA *watches the meeting of father and son.*

Gregori (to Semion). Where do you come from?

Semion. I was at Mr. Kaptchitch's.

Gregori. Well, how is it?

Semion. He asked me to say it was quite impossible for him to come to-day.

Gregori. Very well, I will deliver the message. (*Exit.*)

Scene XXXVIII.

The Same except Gregori.

Semion (*to his father*). Welcome, little father. Uncle Jefim, Uncle Mitri — I salute you. Is all well at home?

Second Peasant. Welcome, Semion!

First Peasant. Welcome, fellow-brother!

Third Peasant. Welcome, boy! How goes it?

Semion (*friendly*). Well, little father, shall we go and drink tea?

Second Peasant. Wait, we want to get through first. Don't you see that we are busy now?

Semion. Well, then, I will wait at the door. (*He goes.*)

Tania (*follows him*). Why didn't you say a word?

Semion. How can I talk here, before all the people? Only have patience; once at tea, and I will talk. (*Exit.*)

SCENE XXXIX.

The Same except SEMION. FEDOR IVANITCH *enters and sits down by the window with a newspaper.*

First Peasant. Well, Sir, how is it with our affair?

Fedor Ivanitch. Have patience, he will come presently, he will soon be ready.

Tania (to Fedor Ivanitch). How do you know, Fedor Ivanitch, that he will soon be ready?

Fedor Ivanitch. O, I know, when the questions are at an end, he reads aloud to himself question and answer.

Tania. Is it really true, then, that one can talk with spirits through a small plate?

Fedor Ivanitch. It must be so.

Tania. How, if they tell him he ought to sign? Will he then really sign?

Fedor Ivanitch. And what do you mean?

Tania. They do not speak in words, do they?

Fedor Ivanitch. In letters. The letter at which they stop, that he makes a note of.

Tania. And at the *séance?* . . .

Scene XL.

The Same and Leonid Fedorovitch.

Leonid Fedorovitch. Well, my dear friends, I cannot; I should very gladly have done it, but it is impossible. If you have the whole sum, that's another thing.

First Peasant. Yes, real-ly, that would surely be better. But the people are weak, it is quite impossible.

Leonid Fedorovitch. I cannot, it is impossible. Here is your paper, I cannot sign it.

Third Peasant. Have mercy, Sir, have mercy!

Second Peasant. How can one act so? It's an insult.

Leonid Fedorovitch. It is not an insult, children. I asked you in the summer: do you want to? Then it's a bargain. You did not want to, now I cannot.

Third Peasant. Sir, have mercy! How are we to live? Our land is small, hardly a hen — not to say anything of cattle — hardly a hen, I say, has room.

(Leonid Fedorovitch *goes and remains standing in the door.*)

SCENE XLI.

The Same. HER LADYSHIP *and the* PHYSICIAN *come downstairs.* VASSILI LEONIDITCH *follows them in a cheerful mood; he puts money in his pocket-book.*

Her Ladyship (*tightly laced, with hat on*).   To be taken internally, then ?

Physician.   To be taken by all means if the symptoms are repeated.   But above all — lead a more sensible life.   How do you expect a thick syrup to pass through a capillary tube if, be-sides, you press the tube together ?   That is impossible!   It is the same with the alimentary canal!   That is surely simple enough.

Her Ladyship.   Yes, indeed, indeed !

Physician.   Indeed, you say, and everything remains the same.   That will not do, your ladyship, that will not do.   Good bye !

Her Ladyship.   Not good bye, but *au revoir !* I shall surely expect you in the evening.   With-out you I cannot come to a decision.

Physician.   Very well, very well, if I have time, I shall come.   (*Exit.*)

Scene XLII.

The Same except the Physician.

Her Ladyship (observing the peasants). What does this mean? What is this? What sort of people are these?

(*The peasants bow.*)

Fedor Ivanitch. They are countrymen from the region of Kursk; they have come to his lordship to buy land.

Her Ladyship. I see they are countrymen, but who admitted them?

Fedor Ivanitch. Leonid Fedorovitch gave orders. He has just talked with them about the sale of the land.

Her Ladyship. What sale? We don't need to sell anything. And above all — how can one admit persons from the street into this house! How can one admit persons from the street! One does not admit persons into the house who have passed the night God knows where. . . . (*She gets more and more excited.*) In their garments, I suppose, every little fold is full of microbes: scarlatina microbes, small-pox microbes, diphtheria microbes! For are they not from Kursk, the province of Kursk, where

diphtheria is epidemic ! . . . Doctor, doctor !
Call the doctor back !

(*Exit* LEONID FEDOROVITCH ; *he locks the door behind
him.—* GREGORI *follows the* PHYSICIAN.)

SCENE XLIII.

The Same except LEONID FEDOROVITCH *and* GREGORI.

Vassili Leoniditch (*blows the cigar-smoke at
the peasants*).   Calm yourself, mamma ; if you
wish, I will smoke them so that all the microbes
will expire.   Well ?

(HER LADYSHIP *is persistently silent ; she awaits the
return of the* PHYSICIAN.)

Vassili Leoniditch (*to the peasants*).   Do you
breed hogs ?   That is a profitable business.

First Peasant.   Real-ly, sometimes we also
raise hogs.

Vassili Leoniditch.   Such . . . i-u . . . i-u
(*He grunts like a sucking pig.*)

Her Ladyship.   Wowó, Wowó !   Stop.

Vassili Leoniditch.   A good pig baby, eh ?

First Peasant.   Real-ly, a good sucking pig.

Her Ladyship.   Wowó, stop, I tell you !

Second Peasant.   What's that for ?

Third Peasant.   I told you in the first place
that we ought meantime to go to our lodgings.

Scene XLIV.

The Same, the PHYSICIAN, *and* GREGORI.

Physician. What's up now? What's the matter.

Her Ladyship. You always say one must not get excited. Now how can one remain calm here? For two whole months I do not visit my sister, and guard myself against every questionable visit. Suddenly I find people from Kursk, straight from Kursk where diphtheria rages, right in my own house!

Physician. Do you mean these splendid fellows?

Her Ladyship. Certainly, right from the diphtheria district.

Physician. Yes, if they are from the diphtheria district, it is indeed careless; but one need not get so excited over it.

Her Ladyship. But you yourself always caution us to be careful!

Physician. Yes, yes, but nevertheless one need not get so excited over it.

Her Ladyship. How can you say that? We must have everything thoroughly disinfected now.

Physician. No, no, why, thoroughly, that is too expensive, that would cost 300 roubles and more. Let me fix it for you. To one large bottle of water . . .

Her Ladyship. Distilled?

Physician. Quite immaterial. Distilled is better — Well, then, to each bottle of water take a tablespoonful of salicylic acid, and have everything washed with it which they in any way have touched ; and these fellows themselves must of course leave. That will suffice. Then you need not fear anything. Of this solution you may also spray two or three glassfuls into the air with the atomizer. You shall see how well everything will be. Quite harmless.

Her Ladyship. Where is Tania ? Call Tania !

SCENE XLV.

The Same and TANIA.

Tania. What does her ladyship wish ?

Her Ladyship. Do you know the big bottle in the wardrobe ?

Tania. With which we sprinkled the wash-woman yesterday ?

Her Ladyship. Yes, that, what other one ?

Take that bottle, then; first wash the spot where they are standing with soap, then . . .

Tania. Very well. I know, I know.

Her Ladyship. Then take the atomizer . . . However, I will come back and do that myself.

Physician. Only do that, and trouble yourself no further. *Au revoir*, now, until evening. (*Exit.*)

SCENE XLVI.

The Same except the PHYSICIAN.

Her Ladyship. And with these away, away, that not a trace of them may remain. Away, away! Go, what are you staring at?

First Peasant. Real-ly, in our ignorance, we were told . . .

Gregori (leading the peasants away). Now, go, go!

Second Peasant. Only let me take my bundle.

Third Peasant. Gracious God! I said at the start—we ought to wait at our lodgings. (*Gregori pushes him out.*)

Scene XLVII.

Her Ladyship, Gregori, Fedor Ivanitch, Tania, Vassili Leoniditch, *and the* Carrier.

Carrier (who has repeatedly attempted to speak). Am I to have an answer?

Her Ladyship. Ah, he from Bourdiet? *(Angrily.)* There is no answer, there is no answer, take it back with you. I told him I did not order such a costume, and I will not allow my daughter to wear it.

Carrier. I know nothing about it; I was sent here.

Her Ladyship. Just go, go, and take it with you again. I will go there myself.

Vassili Leoniditch (solemnly). Sir Messenger of Bourdiet, begone!

Carrier. You might have said that long ago. Was it necessary for me to wait here five hours?!

Vassili Leoniditch. Messenger of Bourdiet, begone!

Her Ladyship. Hush, now, I beg you!

(*Exit* Carrier.)

Scene XLVIII.

The Same except the Carrier.

Her Ladyship. Betsy! Where is she? One must always wait for her.

Vassili Leoniditch (screams at the top of his voice). Betsy! Petristcheff! Come quicker, quicker, quicker! Eh?

Scene XLIX.

The Same, Petristcheff, Betsy, *and* Maria Konstantinovna.

Her Ladyship. One must always wait for you.

Betsy. On the contrary, I am waiting for you.

(Petristcheff *salutes only with a nod of his head and kisses* Her Ladyship's *hand.*)

Her Ladyship. How do you do? (*To Betsy.*) You must always talk back!

Betsy. If you are not in good humor, mamma, I would rather not drive out with you.

Her Ladyship. Are we going to take a drive or not?

Betsy. Say we drive, then ; what else ? .

Her Ladyship. Have you seen what the man from Bourdiet brought ?

Betsy. I have seen it, and I was delighted with it. I ordered the costume, and will wear it when it is paid for.

Her Ladyship. I will not pay for it, and I will not permit you to wear an improper costume.

Betsy. Since when is it improper ? Until now it was proper ; suddenly you have a fit of prudery.

Her Ladyship. No prudery whatever ; if the entire waist is fixed over, it may do.

Betsy. Mamma, that is certainly impossible.

Her Ladyship. Well, get ready.

(*They sit down.* GREGORI *puts on their overshoes.*)

Vassili Leoniditch. Maria Konstantinovna, do you see how empty the hall has become ?

Maria Konstantinovna (*laughing*). What do you mean ?

Vassili Leoniditch. The man from Bourdiet is gone. Eh ? Well ? (*Laughs loud.*)

Her Ladyship. Let us start then. (*She walks towards the door and suddenly returns.*) Tania !

Tania. What does your ladyship wish?

Her Ladyship. That Fifka may not catch cold during my absence. If he should desire to go out, by all means put the yellow cloak around him. He is not quite well.

Tania. Very well, your ladyship.

(*Exeunt* HER LADYSHIP, BETSY, MARIA KONSTANTI-NOVNA, *and* GREGORI.)

SCENE L.

PETRISTCHEFF, VASSILI LEONIDITCH, TANIA, *and* FEDOR IVANITCH.

Petristcheff. Well, how is it? What have you accomplished?

Vassili Leoniditch. I tell you it cost a lot of trouble. First I went to my sire — he growled at me and sent me away. Then, to my mother — there I got it. Here it is. (*He slaps his pocket.*) When I take anything into my head, I am simply irresistible. . . . Hooks of steel! Eh? And now my wolf-killers will of course be brought to-day.

(*Exeunt* PETRISTCHEFF *and* VASSILI LEONIDITCH, *taking their overcoats.* TANIA *follows them.*)

Scene LI.

Fedor Ivanitch *alone.*

Fedor Ivanitch. Continual discord. Why can't they live in peace? Yes, one must admit, the young generation — is after all something different. And the rule of woman? At first Leonid Fedorovitch would gladly have favored the peasants; then he saw her going into hysterics and slammed the door to. A rare good man! Yes, rarely good! . . . What's this? Tania brings them back?

Scene LII.

Fedor Ivanitch, Tania, *and the three peasants.*

Tania. Just come, just come, little uncles, no harm.

Fedor Ivanitch. Why have you brought them here again?

Tania. Pray, dear Fedor Ivanitch, we must surely do something for them. And I will scrub up everything again.

Fedor Ivanitch. Nothing will come of their case; I can see it already.

First Peasant.   Well, Sir, shall we settle our matter ?   If your grace will take a little trouble, we will surely show ourselves richly grateful on behalf of the commune in reward for your trouble.

Third Peasant.   Will you not try, dear Sir ? We cannot live.   Our land is small, hardly a hen — not to say anything of cattle — hardly a hen, I say, has room.

(They bow.)

Fedor Ivanitch.   I really pity you,. but I cannot do anything for you, little friends.   I understand very well, but he has said no.   What's to be done, now ?   Her ladyship also is against it.   Hardly !   But let me have the document ; I will go to him ; I will try ; I will implore him !   *(Exit.)*

Scene LIII.

TANIA *and the three peasants (they sigh).*

Tania.   Now tell me, little uncles, how is it with your affair ?

First Peasant.   Only his signature.

Tania.   His lordship is to sign the document ?

First Peasant.   Only to sign it with his own

hand, and to take his money, and the matter is finished.

Third Peasant. If he only would write! I want, he says, as the peasants want, he says. That's the whole matter. He takes and signs.

Tania. Only to sign? His lordship is only to place his name on the document? (*She meditates.*)

First Peasant. Real-ly, the business depends only on that. That is, when he has signed, there is nothing more to do.

Tania. Just wait, let's see what Fedor Ivanitch brings. If he cannot persuade his lordship, I will try a ruse.

Second Peasant. You will get him to come round?

Tania. I will try.

Third Peasant. Hey, girl, you intend to do something for us? Only carry out the thing, and we will bind ourselves, I say, to support you for life at the expense of the commune. That's a thing!

First Peasant. If you will do us such a turn, we can really set you in gold.

Second Peasant. No doubt about it!

Tania. I will not positively promise it. As they say: one can try . . .

First Peasant. — and a question costs nothing. Real-ly true!

SCENE LIV.

The Same and FEDOR IVANITCH.

Fedor Ivanitch. No, good friends, your business is all up; he said no and sticks to it. Take your document. Go, go!

First Peasant (takes the document. To Tania). So we must after all, so to speak, rely on you.

Tania. Presently, presently. You will now go and wait outdoors; I shall immediately come to you and tell you what's to be done.

(Exeunt peasants.)

SCENE LV.

FEDOR IVANITCH *and* TANIA.

Tania. Fedor Ivanitch, my dear, request his lordship to please come out to me. I have to speak a word to him.

Fedor Ivanitch. What sort of news may that be?

Tania. It must be, Fedor Ivanitch. Just announce it, please; it is nothing bad, God knows.

Fedor Ivanitch.   What can it be?

Tania.   A little secret.   I will betray it later. Only announce it.

Fedor Ivanitch (smiling).   I cannot understand what you are driving at!   But very well, I will say it, I will say it.   *(Exit.)*

SCENE LVI.

TANIA *(alone)*.

Tania.   I declare, it must succeed.   Didn't he say himself that Semion had the force, and don't I know how everything is to be managed? Then nobody suspected anything.   Now I am going to bring Semion up to it.   And if it does not succeed, there is no harm done.   Is that a sin?

SCENE LVII.

TANIA, LEONID FEDOROVITCH, *later* FEDOR IVANITCH.

Leonid Fedorovitch (smiling).   A strange petitioner!   What is it about?

Tania.   A little secret, Leonid Fedorovitch. Permit me to tell you under four eyes.

Leonid Fedorovitch.   What can that be? Fedor, leave us a moment.

SCENE LVIII.

LEONID FEDOROVITCH *and* TANIA.

Tania. Leonid Fedorovitch, I have been brought up in your house from a child; I am grateful to you for everything, and I want to speak openly to you as to my own father. Semion, who is in your house, wants to marry me.

Leonid Fedorovitch. Was that it?

Tania. I speak as openly to you as to God. I have nobody with whom I could consult; for I am an orphan.

Leonid Fedorovitch. Well, why not? He is really a good boy.

Tania. Certainly, he would be real nice; only one thing seems doubtful to me. And I wanted to ask you, there is something in him, I do not quite understand it . . . If it should be anything bad!

Leonid Fedorovitch. What, does he drink?

Tania. No, God forbid! But I know that there is a Spirituism . . .

Leonid Fedorovitch. You know that?

Tania. Why shouldn't I? I understand very well. Others with their lack of education don't perhaps understand . . .

Leonid Fedorovitch.   Well, what then ?

Tania.   I am anxious about Semion.   It happens with him —

Leonid Fedorovitch.   What happens ?

Tania.   Something like Spirituism.   Just ask the domestics.   As soon as he goes to sleep at the table, right away the table begins to tremble and to squeak : tuk, tu ... tuk!   All the domestics have heard it.

Leonid Fedorovitch.   Exactly what I told Sergei Ivanovitch this morning.   And ?

Tania.   And ... when was it ?   Yes, Wednesday.   We had just sat down to dinner.   Scarcely had he sat down at the table when the spoon jumped into his hand all of its own accord — hop!

Leonid Fedorovitch.   Ah, that is interesting!   Hop — into his hand?   How, had he gone to sleep?

Tania.   I didn't notice.   I think he had gone to sleep.

Leonid Fedorovitch.   Well, and?

Tania.   Well, I am anxious, and wanted to ask you whether any harm could come from it ?   To have to be together with some one for a whole life, if something like that is in him ...

Leonid Fedorovitch (*smiling*).   No, no, don't

be afraid ; there's nothing bad in that. That
only means that he is a *medium*, simply a medium. I knew long ago that he was a medium.

Tania. Strange ! ... And I have been in
such fear !

Leonid Fedorovitch. No, no, fear nothing,
that is of no consequence. (*To himself.*) That
is excellent. Kaptchitch can't come, so we can
make experiments with him this very day. . . .
No, no, fear nothing, my child, he will also be
a good husband and everything . . . That is an
especial power, which all men possess. It is
only weaker in some and stronger in others.

Tania. I thank you with all my heart. I
shall not think of it any more now. And I
have had such fear about it. That comes from
our ignorance.

Leonid Fedorovitch. No, no, don't be afraid,
Tania !

SCENE LIX.

The Same and FEDOR IVANITCH.

Leonid Fedorovitch. I am going out. To
prepare everything for this evening's *séance.*

Fedor Ivanitch. But Mr. Kaptchitch is not
coming to-day.

Leonid Fedorovitch. No matter, it's all the

same. (*He puts on his cloak.*) We shall have a trial *séance* with our own medium.

(*Exit.* FEDOR IVANITCH *goes out with him.*)

SCENE LX.

TANIA *alone.*

Tania. He believed it, he believed it (*she squeals and jumps*). Sure as God, he believed it! A real miracle (*she squeals*). Now the thing must succeed, if only Semion doesn't get frightened.

SCENE LXI.

TANIA *and* FEDOR IVANITCH (*coming back*).

Fedor Ivanitch. Well, how is it, did you tell your secret?

Tania. Certainly. I will tell you about it, too; only later. But I have a favor to ask of you also, Fedor Ivanitch.

Fedor Ivanitch. What sort of a favor can that be?

Tania (*ashamed*). You have always been like a second father to me. I will speak to you openly, as to God.

Fedor Ivanitch. No flattery now; say right out what you want.

Tania. What I want? I want — Semion wants to marry me.

Fedor Ivanitch. That's it! That's why I have noticed . . .

Tania. Why should I conceal it? I am an orphan, and you know how it is here in this city life; everybody is after a girl; be it only Gregori Michailitch. I have no peace from him. That one also — you know? They act as if I were a lifeless being, as if I were here only for their pleasure . . .

Fedor Ivanitch. Clever girl, bravo! Well, what is it then?

Tania. Semion has written to his father, and now he has seen me, the father I mean, immediately he says: He has come to be a fine gentleman! The son I mean, Fedor Ivanitch! (*She makes a bow.*) Take the place of a father to me. Speak to the old man, to Semion's father. I will take them to the kitchen; then you will come in and speak to the old man.

Fedor Ivanitch (*smiling*). That is, I am to be your match-maker? Very well, that may be.

Tania. Dearest, best Fedor Ivanitch, take the place of a father to me, and I will pray for you all my life.

66

68 *The Fruits of Culture*

Fedor Ivanitch. Well, well, I will go. Rely on me. (*He takes his paper.*)

Tania. You will be a second father to me.

Fedor Ivanitch. Very well, very well.

Tania. I may hope then ... (*Exit.*)

SCENE LXII.

FEDOR IVANITCH *alone.*

Fedor Ivanitch (sways his head to and fro). A winning, good child! How many such are ruined, sad! One single false step, then they go from hand to hand . . Not a soul to draw them from the mire. How miserably that darling Natalie fared! . . . She was also good, she also had a mother who cherished and cared for her, and had reared her ... (*Takes his paper.*) Well, how is it with our Ferdinand? How is he going to disentangle himself? . . .

(*The curtain falls.*)

ACT II.

*The stage represents the interior of the domestics'
kitchen. The peasants, in shirt-sleeves and reeking with
perspiration, are sitting at the table and drinking tea.*
FEDOR IVANITCH *is smoking a cigar on the other side of
the stage. On the stove lies the* OLD COOK, *who is not
seen during the first four scenes.*

SCENE I.

The three peasants and FEDOR IVANITCH.

Fedor Ivanitch. My advice is to let him have
his will. If he wishes it and she also, then let
them. The girl is good and honest. That she
likes to dress up, don't mind that too much.
That's the way it is in the city ; it wouldn't do
else. And the girl is clever.

Second Peasant. Well, if he insists on it.
He has to marry her, not I. But she is already
much too fine. What are we to do with her in
a peasant's hut ? Her mother-in-law will not
even be allowed to caress her.

Fedor Ivanitch. That has nothing to do
with being fine, good friend, but with character.

If she has a good character, then she will also be obedient and respectful.

Second Peasant. Well, I'll not withhold my consent, if the boy has set his mind on the girl. It's bad, anyway, to take one whom one doesn't love. I'll consult with my old woman, and then as God wills!

Fedor Ivanitch. Well then, shake hands on it.

Second Peasant. I suppose it's fate.

First Peasant. What luck you have, Sachar! You come here to settle some business, and just see — he takes away a princess for his daughter-in-law. Now we'll only have to wet it yet, so to speak ; then it's as it ought to be.

Fedor Ivanitch. Not necessary at all.

(Uncomfortable silence.)

Fedor Ivanitch. You see, I can appreciate the life of the peasants. I am thinking myself, I tell you, of buying a piece of land. I would like to build me a house, and farm. Perhaps even in your neighborhood.

Second Peasant. That is very nice!

First Peasant. Real-ly, with a little money one can provide himself with every pleasure in the country.

Third Peasant. Why say anything about it? In the country, I say, there is in any case more freedom; quite different from the city.

Fedor Ivanitch. How, will you admit me to your commune, if I should settle down amongst you?

Second Peasant. Why shouldn't we admit you? You drink with the elders and are admitted.

First Peasant. Yes, you can open a bar, so to speak, or an eating-house. What a life that would be! One need not die at all then. You'll be the gentleman, and need ask nobody's pleasure.

Fedor Ivanitch. We'll see, we'll see. I merely wish to lead a quiet life in my old age. I am having a good enough time here — nor will it come easy to me to leave; Leonid Fedorovitch is, indeed, a rarely good man.

First Peasant. That is really so. But why does he treat our business in that way? Is it to remain this way without a result?

Fedor Ivanitch. He would like to!

Second Peasant. Is he afraid of his wife?

Fedor Ivanitch. He is not afraid of her; but neither will she give her consent.

Third Peasant. If you would put in a word

for us, little father? How are we to live otherwise? Our land is small . . .

Fedor Ivanitch. First let us wait and see
what Tatiana will bring about with her en-
deavors. She has taken it in hand, has she
not?

Third Peasant. Little father, have mercy on
us! Our land is small, hardly a hen — not to
say anything of cattle — hardly a hen, I say,
has room.

Fedor Ivanitch. Yes, if it depended on me.
(*To the second peasant.*) So it is settled, then,
good friend, we two are now fathers-in-law.
The affair with Tania is agreed to?

Second Peasant. If I have said it once, I
don't take back my word, even without having
wet it. If our affair would only succeed.

Scene II.

The Same. The Cook *enters, casts a glance at the
stove, makes a sign, and begins at once to talk viva-
ciously with* Fedor Ivanitch.

Cook. They have just called up Semion from
their lordship's kitchen; his lordship and he
who conjures with him, that baldhead; they
put him on a chair and commanded him to take
part, in the place of Kaptchitch.

Fedor Ivanitch. What lie is that?

Cook. Sure. Just now Jacob told Tania about it.

Fedor Ivanitch. Strange!

SCENE III.

The Same and the COACHMAN.

Fedor Ivanitch. What do you want?

Coachman (to Fedor Ivanitch). Tell their lordships I did not come into their service in order to house with dogs. Let who will do that. I don't feel like living with dogs.

Fedor Ivanitch. With what dogs?

Coachman. They've sent three curs to us in the coachmen's room from Vassili Leoniditch. They've soiled everything, and howl, and one dare not touch them — they bite at you. Mad beasts! — they'll eat one up before one knows it. And I would just like to smash their legs with a club.

Fedor Ivanitch. When was that?

Coachman. To-day they brought them from the exposition, expensive rat-hounds or whatever they are. The devil knows what they are called. Either the dogs must leave the coachmen's room or the coachmen. You may tell that to their lordships.

Fedor Ivanitch. Yes, that is no way of doing. I will go upstairs and ask.

Coachman. They can come down here to Lukeria. What ?

Cook (enraged). Here human beings have to eat, and you want to shut up the curs in here ? It is already . . .

Coachman. And in my place there are coats, straps, and harnesses. And cleanliness is expected of me. Perhaps in the butler's room ?

Fedor Ivanitch. I must speak to Vassili Leoniditch.

Coachman (annoyed). Let him have the curs fastened to his neck and run about with them. He likes to drive about all day anyway. Hector he has ruined out and out. And what a horse he was ! . . . O such a life ! (*Exit, slamming the door.*)

SCENE IV.

The Same except the COACHMAN.

Fedor Ivanitch. Yes, bad management, bad management. (*To the peasants.*) It's settled then ; meanwhile good bye, children !

Peasants. God be with you !

(*Exit* FEDOR IVANITCH.)

SCENE V.

The Same except FEDOR IVANITCH. *As soon as* FEDOR IVANITCH *leaves, groans are heard in the direction of the stove.*

Second Peasant. A fine gentleman, like a general!

Cook. Nothing special! His own room, free washing from their lordships, his tea, his sugar, —everything he gets from their lordships, and food from their lordships' table.

The Old Cook. The devil, too — and why shouldn't he be doing finely? He steals like a magpie!

Second Peasant. Who is that — the fellow on the stove?

Cook. He — an old man. (*Pause.*)

First Peasant. I have seen you eating before, too; you must be rich people.

Cook. We have no reason to complain. As to that matter, she is not miserly; Sundays wheat bread, fish during Lent and the holidays, and whoever doesn't want to needn't fast at all.

Second Peasant. Does anybody eat other things on fast days, then?

Cook. Well, all do. Only the coachman (not the one who was here, but the old one), and Semion, and I, and the housekeeper — we fast; all the others eat meat.

Second Peasant.   And he himself?

Cook.   Ah! there you make a fine mistake. He scarcely remembers any more that there is a fast day.

Third Peasant.   Gracious God!

First Peasant.   That's the way it is among great folks; they learn that out of books. That's culture!

Third Peasant.   Every day, I think, they have wheat bread?

Cook.   Bah! wheat bread.   They care a lot for your wheat bread!   You ought just to see for once what they do eat!   All the things that are served on their table!

First Peasant.   What great folks eat, that — we know — is light as air!

Cook.   Good! air! — well, they fall to pretty lively!

First Peasant.   With an appetite, so to speak.

Cook.   Because they also drink with it. These sweet wines, whiskeys, effervescing drinks, for every course a special one.   They eat and drink, and eat and drink again . . .

First Peasant.   It is so arranged beforehand that they may eat all the more.

Cook. Yes, bless me, how they do feed! With them it is not like this: sit down, eat, cross one's self, get up,— they eat without interruption.

Second Peasant. Like hogs — with the feet in the trough. (*Peasants laugh.*)

Cook. Scarcely have they opened their eyes, praise the Lord, directly they call for the samovar, tea, coffee, chocolate. When they have emptied two samovars — go, fetch the third. Then immediately breakfast, immediately dinner, and then immediately coffee again; scarcely have they filled their stomachs — immediately again tea; then all sorts of trifles: sweetmeats, dessert,— and so on without end. When they go to bed, they are still eating.

Third Peasant. Yes, so it is. (*Laughs.*)

First and Second Peasants. What are you laughing for?

Third Peasant. I should for once like to live a day like that, too.

Second Peasant. When do they do their work, anyway?

Cook. What work have *they* to do? Cards, piano,— that is their work. The young lady, when she just opens her eyes, off she goes for the piano — and thumps away on it! And the other, the teacher, who lives in the house, is already standing there and waiting for the piano to become free; when the one is through, dash — the other pounces down on it. Sometimes they get two pianos, two sit down to each one, and then four drum away at once. They drum away, I tell you, till one can hear it down here.

Third Peasant. Ah, gracious God!

Cook. That is their work: piano and cards. When they meet, right away it's cards, wine, cigars, and so it goes through the whole night. Scarcely are they up in the morning, it's eating again.

SCENE VI.

The Same and SEMION.

Semion. I wish you a good dinner.

First Peasant. Please sit down.

Semion (approaches the table). Thank you very much. (*The first peasant pours him some tea.*)

Second Peasant. Where have you been?

Semion. I have been upstairs.

Second Peasant. Well, what are they doing there?

Semion. I don't understand anything about it. I don't know what they call it.

Second Peasant. Well, but what are they doing, anyhow?

Semion. But I don't know what it's called. They tried to find a force in me. But I don't understand anything about it. Tatiana says: Go on, she says, and we'll get the land for our peasants; he'll surely give it.

Second Peasant. How does she expect to bring that round?

Semion. I don't understand her; she won't tell. Only do as I tell you, she says.

Second Peasant. Do what?

Semion. First nothing. They made me sit on a chair, put out the light, and told me to go to sleep. And Tatiana hid herself near by. They cannot see her, but I see her.

Second Peasant. What's the good of that?

Semion. God knows, I don't.

First Peasant. Surely — to kill time.

Second Peasant. I can see, we two will never make sense of that. Tell us rather, did you save much money?

Semion. I didn't get any. It was all spent for me. It might amount to 28 roubles.

Second Peasant. Very well, and if with God's help we complete the purchase, I will take you home with us, Semka.

Semion. With pleasure.

Second Peasant. You have become, I think, a fine gentleman. You won't want to do farm work?

Semion. Farm work? On the spot. Mowing, ploughing, nothing will go against my hand.

First Peasant. You won't feel like returning to city life, so to speak?

Semion. No, one can live in the country, too.

First Peasant. Uncle Mitri is already on the lookout for your place for the fine living.

Semion. Well, Uncle Mitri will soon enough get tired of it. First it looks easy, but you'll soon see there is plenty of running to do, and then one's in for it.

Cook. O Uncle Mitri, if you were only to attend their balls for once! How you would open your eyes!

Third Peasant. There they never stop eating at all!

Cook. What are you thinking about? You ought just to see that! Fedor Ivanitch took me along once. I look about: the ladies — splendid! Dressed up, dressed up — one cannot imagine it. And naked down to here — and the arms naked!

Third Peasant. Gracious God!

Second Peasant. Fie, low!

First Peasant. That is to say, the climate permits of that.

Cook. And I look and look, little uncle: what does that mean? all naked bodies. Would you believe it? Old ones, our lady — she has grand-children, you must know — also naked.

Third Peasant. Gracious God!

Cook. And then: when the music starts up and plays, every gentleman goes to his lady, embraces her, and then they whirl round in a circle.

Second Peasant. The old ones too?

Cook. The old ones, too.

Semion. No, the old ones remain sitting.

Cook. You say that; I myself have seen it.

Semion. But it isn't true.

Old Cook (raising his head, hoarse). That is polka-mazurka. Eh, you are stupid. You don't know that. They dance so ...

Cook. You, dancer, keep your mouth shut, do you know. Pst! somebody is coming.

Scene VII.

The Same and Gregori.   *The* Old Cook *hides himself quickly.*

Gregori (to the Cook).   Get sauerkraut !

Cook.   I've just come from the cellar, now I must run right down again.   For whom ?

Gregori.   A cooling dish for the young ladies. Quick !   Sitting here with Semion, and I don't know where to run to first.

Cook.   First they fill themselves up with the sweet stuff, until nothing more will go down ; then they get a taste for sauerkraut.

First Peasant.   That's for cleaning out the stomach, so to speak.

Cook.   Well, when there is room, they begin to fill up again.   (*She takes a dish and goes away.*)

Scene VIII.

The Same except the Cook.

Gregori (to the peasants).   Now just see : how comfortable they made themselves.   You better look out !   If her ladyship should hear of it, she will raise a terrible storm, worse than this morning.   (*Laughs and goes away.*)

SCENE IX. ·

The three peasants, SEMION, *and the* OLD COOK (*on the stove*).

First Peasant. Real-ly, she raised a fine hail storm a while ago — awful!

Second Peasant. It's plain, first he was for us, then when he saw she was taking the roof off the house, he slammed the door to. You may go to the devil, he thinks.

Third Peasant (*with a movement of the hand*). The same story the world over. My old woman, too, I say, when she gets into a rage,— God save us! Then I leave the house of my own accord. The deuce take her! One is glad if she doesn't go for one with the iron poker. Gracious God!

SCENE X.

The Same and JACOB (*rushes in with a prescription in his hand*).

Jacob. Semion, hurry to the apothecary, quick, get these powders for her ladyship.

Semion. But he told me to stay here.

Jacob. There is time enough. Your turn

doesn't come till after tea . . . I wish you a good dinner !

First Peasant.   Please sit down.

(*Exit* SEMION.)

SCENE XI.

The Same except SEMION.

Jacob.   I have no time ; well, just a drop, for company's sake !

First Peasant.   We are here holding a conversation about how haughty her ladyship was a while ago.

Jacob.   O, she is hot-tempered !   So hot-tempered that she gets quite beside herself. Sometimes she cries in a rage.

First Peasant.   What I was going to ask, so to speak.   She was all the time talking about macrotes.   Macrotes, macrotes, she says, they brought macrotes into the house.   What use are these macrotes put to, anyhow?

Jacob.   Ah, you mean the macrobes.   That is, they say, a kind of bugs from which all diseases are said to spring.   You see you are suspected of having some.   And the place where you have been has been scrubbed and scrubbed, and sprinkled and sprinkled. There is a medicine from which they perish, these little bugs.

Second Peasant. But then whereabouts on us are they, these little bugs.

Jacob (drinks tea). People say they are so, so small that one can't see them, even under a glass.

Second Peasant. How does she know then that there are some on me? Perhaps she's got more of these filthy things than I?

Jacob. Go ask her yourself!

Second Peasant. And I think it's all empty talk.

Jacob. Certainly, empty talk; but the doctors must invent something, what should they be paid for else? Every day he comes driving up to us. Walks in, says something — pockets ten roubles.

Second Peasant. Impossible!

Jacob. There's one even who gets a — hundred.

First Peasant. What? A hundred?

Jacob. A hundred? You say: a hundred? — A thousand one must give when he goes into the country. If you will give a thousand, he says, well; if not, die!

Third Peasant. Gracious God!

Second Peasant. How, has he some magic word?

Jacob. Must be. Once I was with a general in the neighborhood of Moscow, a bad, proud gentleman, the general, terrible! One day his little daughter got sick. They get the thousand roubles at once — and I come . . . They all agreed, and he came. Then something was not done right for him. O, I tell you, how he pounces down on the general! Ah! says he, that is the respect you have for me, that is the respect. Very well, cure your child yourself! — What do you think? The general forgot his pride and flattered him in every way: little father, do not desert us!

First Peasant. And he got the thousand roubles?

Jacob. What else, do you think?

Second Peasant. Ridiculously much money! What could not we peasants do with so much money!

Third Peasant. And I think it's all bosh. When I got footsore that time — I doctored and doctored, five roubles' worth I doctored. Then I stopped doctoring — and my foot was well.

(*The* OLD COOK *on the stove coughs.*)

Jacob. Back again, little friend ?

First Peasant. What's he ?

Jacob. He used to be our master's cook ; he comes to see Lukeria.

First Peasant. That is to say, head cook. What, does he live here ?

Jacob. N—n—no ! He is not allowed to be here. He doesn't live anywhere : one day here, the next there. When he's got a half-penny, he goes to a night shelter ; when he's spent his money in drink, he comes here.

Second Peasant. How could he get into such a way ?

Jacob. He degenerated. And what a man he was — a gentleman ! A gold watch he carried, he got forty roubles a month, and now, but for Lukeria, he would have long ago died of hunger.

SCENE XII.

The Same and the COOK *(with sauerkraut).*

Jacob (to Lukeria). As I see, Pavel Petrovitch is back again.

Cook. Where is he to stay, then — shall he freeze to death, what ?

Third Peasant. What whiskey does ! Yes, whiskey . . . (*He smacks his lips in sympathy.*)

Second Peasant. It's well-known : if a man is firm, he is firmer than a rock; if he is weak, he is weaker than water.

The Old Cook (gets down from the stove with his hands and feet trembling). See here, Lukeria, give me a small glass.

Cook. Where are you crawling to? I will give you such a glass! . . .

Old Cook. Do you not fear God? I am dying! Good friends, a nickel!

Cook. See here, hurry, and get back on the stove.

Old Cook. Cook! A small h-ha-half glass. For Christ's sake, do you hear, do you understand me — I implore you in Christ's name.

Cook. Go, go! You can have tea!

Old Cook. Your tea, your tea! An insipid drink, it has no strength. Only a drop of — brandy — Lukeria!

Third Peasant. Ah, little friend, how he suffers!

Second Peasant. Give him some; what of it?

Cook (goes to the cupboard and pours him a small glass). There, take! No more though!

Old Cook (grasps it and drinks trembling). Lukeria, cook! I drink it, and you must know . . .

Cook. Well, well, don't talk! Climb back on the stove, and don't stir!

(*The* OLD COOK *climbs humbly on the stove and does not cease mumbling to himself.*)

Second Peasant. What it means when a man's weak!

• *First Peasant.* Real-ly — human weakness!

Third Peasant. What can one say about it?

(*The* OLD COOK *stretches himself, and is still mumbling. Pause.*)

Second Peasant. What I was further going to ask: The girl here in your house, the one from our place, Axinia's girl — how is it with her, how? What kind of a life is she leading — that is to say, is she respectable?

Jacob. A good girl; one must speak well of her.

Cook. I will tell you the truth, little uncle, I know all about the life here; do you want to take Tatiana for your son — then quick before she comes to grief; for that is sure to come.

Jacob. Yes, that is really so. In the summer there was a girl with us, Natalie; she was a good girl, and she was ruined for nothing, worse than this one. . . . (*He points to the Old Cook.*)

Cook. Thousands of us are ruined here, whole villages of us. Everybody is enticed by the easy work and the good eating. . . . And with the good eating — you see — it goes down hill quickly. And when she is down, then they don't need such a one any more. Away with her at once — let's have a new one. It was so with that dear Natalie — she was down — she was driven away at once. She gave birth and was taken sick, and last spring she died in the hospital. And what a girl that was!

Third Peasant. Gracious God! Weak creatures. They are to be pitied.

Old Cook. Yes, they pity us, those vermin! (*He dangles his legs down from the stove.*) For thirty years I roasted myself at the heat — then they had no use for me any more, die like a dog! . . . Yes, they pity one!

First Peasant. Real-ly true, so goes the world!

Second Peasant. As long as they are eating and drinking, you are their good fellow. When they have eaten enough and drunk enough — begone, filthy dog!

Third Peasant. Gracious God!

Old Cook. You know a heap. What is: *Szotié à la bomong?* What is: *Bavassari?*

How much I used to know! Just think of it! The Czar has eaten the work of my hands. Now those vermin don't need me any more! But they won't down me!

Cook. Well, well, his tongue has begun to wag. Go to the . . . ! Go crawl into your corner, that they won't see you. If Fedor Ivanitch or some of the others should come, they'll chase you and me both out of the house.

(*Pause.*)

Jacob. Do you also know my part of the country, Wosnessenskoie?

Second Peasant. To be sure we know it, seventeen versts from us; it's no further, and across the river still less. What are you doing? Have you rented land?

Jacob. My brother is a tenant, and I send him help. Although I am here myself, I am all the time thinking of home.

First Peasant. Real-ly.

Second Peasant. So Anissim is your brother?

Jacob. Certainly, my own brother. At the other end.

Second Peasant. O, I know — the third house.

Scene XIII.

The Same and Tania.

Tania. Jacob Ivanitch! Why do you take things easy down here? You are called!

Jacob. Directly! What's the matter?

Tania. Fifka is barking! He wants something to eat. And she is scolding about you: what a rascal he is, she says, he has no pity, she says, it was time long ago to give the dog his dinner, and he doesn't come! . . . (*She laughs.*)

Jacob (*about to go*). Ò, is she mad? I hope there won't be a row!

Cook (*to Jacob*). Why don't you take the sauerkraut along?

Jacob. Give it to me, give it to me. (*He takes the sauerkraut and goes.*)

Scene XIV.

The Same except Jacob.

First Peasant. Who is to eat dinner now?

Tania. The dog. Her dog. . . . (*She sits down beside them and takes the teapot.*) Is there some tea there still?—if not, I've brought some with me. (*She pours tea.*)

Second Peasant. The dog must eat dinner?

Tania. Certainly! A special chop is prepared for him, that it may not be too fat. I wash his clothes for him, for the dog.

Third Peasant. Gracious God!

Tania. Just like the master who had a funeral for his dog.

Second Peasant. What's that story?

Tania. Listen — a man told it — a certain lord's dog had died. In the midst of the winter he drove out to bury him; buries him, drives back, and weeps. There was a real sharp frost, the coachman's nose trickles, and he wipes it. . . . Let me have your glasses! (*Pours out tea.*) It trickles and trickles, and he keeps on wiping. The master sees it: "How," says he, "why are you weeping?" And the coachman says: "Why, Sir, why shouldn't I weep? What a dog that was!" (*She laughs.*)

Second Peasant. And to himself I suppose he was thinking: If it had been you who kicked the bucket, I shouldn't cry either. . . . (*He laughs.*)

Old Cook (from the stove). That's so, sure!

Tania. Very well, the master returns home, straight he goes to his wife: "How good," says he, "our coachman is, he wept the whole way

—so sorry was he for my Ami." Have him called: "There you shall have some whiskey, and here as a reward — a rouble." She is just like that, and is angry if Jacob has no pity for the dog.

(*The peasants laugh.*)

First Peasant.   Very good!

Second Peasant.   Well, indeed!

Third Peasant.   I declare, girl, you're witty!

Tania (*pours more tea*).   Drink some more! Yes, so it is, one thinks this sort of life so fine, when it is disgusting to clean away all their filth.   Fi!   In the country it is better.

(*The peasants turn up their cups again, which they had turned down.*)

Tania (*pours tea*).   Drink, may it do you good, Jefim Antonitch!   Let me help you to some, Mitri Vlassievitch!

Third Peasant.   Well, then, fill up, fill up.

First Peasant.   Now tell me, sly little puss, does our affair progress?

Tania.   O, it progresses . . .

First Peasant.   Semion has told . . .

Tania (*quickly*).   Told?

Second Peasant.   But one can't understand him.

Tania. I can't say anything at all now, but I'll fix it, I'll fix it. Look here — here is your paper, too! (*She points to the paper under her apron.*) If only the one stroke would succeed. . . . (*She squeals.*) O, how nice that would be!

Second Peasant. Only look out, though, that you don't lose the paper. It has cost money.

Tania. Be quite at your ease. The chief thing is, isn't it, that he signs it?

Third Peasant. Why, what else? His signature and — everything is done. (*He turns down his cup.*) Enough.

Tania (*to herself*). He'll sign, you will see, he'll sign. Drink some more. (*She pours tea.*)

First Peasant. If you'll only bring about the completion of the sale, we will marry you at the expense of the village. (*He declines the tea.*)

Tania (*pours tea and passes the cups*). Drink!

Third Peasant. Just carry it out! And we'll marry you, I say, and I will dance at your wedding. Although I have not danced in my whole life, I will dance then!

Tania (*laughs*). That I hope will come true. (*Pause.*)

Second Peasant (*looking at Tania*). Yes, that's all very fine; but you are not fit for peasants' work.

Tania. I not fit? What, do you think I have no strength? You ought to see me pull her ladyship together; no peasant could pull harder.

Second Peasant. Where do you pull her to, then?

Tania. It is made of whalebone, like a little jacket, down to here. And it is pulled together with strings, as in harnessing up; one must even spit on one's hands.

Second Peasant. That is to say, you lace her tight?

Tania. Yes, yes, I lace her tight. And one surely cannot prop one's feet against her. (*She laughs.*)

Second Peasant. But why do you pull her together?

Tania. So, that's why.

Second Peasant. What, has she taken a vow, or what?

Tania. No, no, for beauty.

First Peasant. You pull her paunch together, so to speak, for beauty's sake?

Tania. One pulls and pulls until her eyes start from their sockets, and still she says: "More." One draws blisters on one's hands; and you say I have no strength!

(*The peasants laugh and wag their heads.*)

Tania. But here I sit and talk. (*She runs away laughing.*)

Third Peasant. That's what I call a girl, she's witty!

First Peasant. And how accurate she is!

Second Peasant. O, yes!

Scene XV.

The three peasants, the Cook, *the* Old Cook (*on the stove*), Sachatoff *and* Vassili Leoniditch *coming.* Sachatoff *holding a teaspoon in his hand.*

Vassili Leoniditch. Not exactly a dinner, but a *déjeuner dinatoire.* And I tell you, it was a splendid breakfast: ham of young pig — delicious! One dines exquisitely at Roulliet's. I have just now come. (*Observing the peasants.*) And the peasants are here again.

Sachatoff. Yes, yes, that is all very fine; but we came here to hide something. Where shall we hide it?

Vassili Leoniditch. Pardon, a moment. (*To the Cook.*) Where are the dogs?

Cook. In the coachmen's room. They are surely not to be taken into the domestics' room?

Vassili Leoniditch. Ah, in the coachmen's room? Very well.

Sachatoff. I am waiting.

Vassili Leoniditch. Pardon, pardon. What, now? Conceal something? You know, Sergei Ivanovitch, I'll tell you something: in the pocket of a peasant, one of these here. Say this one. You there. Where is your pocket?

Third Peasant. What do you want of my pocket? Just think, my pocket he wants! I have money in my pocket.

Sachatoff. Well, where is your little purse?

Third Peasant. What's that to you?

Cook. What are you doing? That's the young gentleman.

Vassili Leoniditch (laughs). Do you know why he is so frightened? I'll tell you: he's got a lot of money in his pocket. Eh?

Sachatoff. Yes, yes, I understand. Well then: You talk to him, meantime I'll slip it into this bag — so that they themselves won't know and can't show him. Talk to them.

Vassili Leoniditch. Right away, right away. Well, how is it, children, will you buy the land? Eh?

First Peasant. We, we want to with our whole heart. But the affair don't get on.

Vassili Leoniditch. You must only not be miserly. Land — is an important thing. I have already told you — mint. One can raise tobacco, too.

First Peasant. Yes, real·ly, all products.

Third Peasant. And you, little father, do put in a good word for us. How can we live? The land is small — not even a hen, I say, has room.

Sachatoff (has slipped the spoon into the bag of the third peasant). C'est fait. Done. Let us go. (*Exit.*)

Vassili Leoniditch. Remember not to be miserly. Ah? Well, good bye! (*Exit.*)

Scene XVI.

The three peasants, the Cook, *and the* Old Cook (*on the stove*).

First Peasant. I said at the start: to our lodgings. For a dime, I say, each of us could have had a room, and we would at least have had peace; here, God save us. Hand out your money, he says. What does that mean?

Second Peasant. He surely has been drinking.

(*The peasants turn down their cups, rise, and cross themselves.*)

First Peasant. Just think, how smart, what he said about the mint that we ought to sow. That one must understand.

Second Peasant. To sow mint, as if that were such an easy matter. Just try it once, strain your back at it, and you will soon get sick of mint. . . . No, thank you! Now say, little sly-boots, where are we to sleep here?

Cook. Lie down — one of you on the stove, the others each on a bench.

Third Peasant. Christ my Saviour. (*He prays.*)

First Peasant. God prosper our business! (*He lies down.*) To-morrow afternoon we might leave on the railroad; Tuesday we are home.

Second Peasant. Will you put out the light?

Cook. How so, put out? Don't they all come running: the one wanting this, the other that. . . . However, only lie down; I'll turn it down.

Second Peasant. How can one make both ends meet on the small strip of land? Ever since Christmas I've been obliged to buy grain. And the oat straw is giving out. So I might take four desjatines myself, have Semion come home.

First Peasant. You have a family. No

trouble on that score! You çan till the land if you only get it. If only our business might end fortunately!

Third Peasant. We must pray to the holy virgin. Perhaps she will have mercy.

Scene XVII.

Quiet; sighing. Then steps are heard, voices, the door is thrown wide open, and in rush GROSSMANN, *blindfolded,* SACHATOFF, *whom* GROSSMANN *is holding by the hand, the* PROFESSOR *and the* PHYSICIAN, *the* FAT LADY *and* LEONID FEDOROVITCH, BETSY *and* PETRISTCHEFF, VASSILI LEONIDITCH *and* MARIA KONSTANTINOVNA, HER LADYSHIP *and the* BARONESS, FEDOR IVANITCH *and* TANIA. *The three peasants, the* COOK *and the* OLD COOK (*invisible*).— *The peasants jump up.—* GROSSMANN *enters with quick steps and remains standing.*

Fat Lady. Don't fear, I'll watch, I have taken it upon myself to watch, and will do my duty strictly. Sergei Ivanovitch, you are not leading him?

Sachatoff. No, no.

Fat Lady. Do not lead him, but follow him willingly. (*To Leonid Fedorovitch.*) I know these experiments. I have made them myself. I feel a twitching, and the same moment . . .

Leonid Fedorovitch. Pardon me, but I must
ask you to keep perfect quiet.   .

Fat Lady. O, yes, I understand that very
well. I have experienced that myself. As
soon as the attention was drawn off, I could no
longer . . .

Leonid Fedorovitch. 'Sh, 'sh . . .

(*They walk about, make search near the first and second peasants, and approach the third.*— GROSS-
MANN *stumbles over a bench.*)

Baroness. *Mais dites-moi, on le paye?*

Her Ladyship. *Je ne saurais vous dire.*

Baroness. *Mais, c'est un monsieur?*

Her Ladyship. *Oh, oui!*

Baroness. *Ça tient du miraculeux. N'est-ce
pas? Comment est-ce qu'il trouve?*

Her Ladyship. *Je ne saurais vous dire.
Mon mari vous l'expliquera.* (*She sees the
peasants and looks for the Cook.*) Pardon.
What is this?

(*The* BARONESS *approaches the group.*)

Her Ladyship (*to the Cook*). Who admitted
the peasants?

Cook. Jacob brought them here.

Her Ladyship. Who told Jacob to?

Cook. I don't know. Fedor Ivanitch saw
them.

Her Ladyship. Leonid!

(LEONID FEDOROVITCH *does not hear; he is absorbed in the search, and hisses for silence.*)

Her Ladyship. Fedor Ivanitch! What does this mean? Did you not see that I disinfected the whole hall, and now they have infected the whole kitchen, the black bread, the *kvass*. . . .

Fedor Ivanitch. I did not think it was dangerous here. And the men are here on business. They come from far away, from my home.

Her Ladyship. That's just it, from the region of Kursk, where people are dying like flies of diphtheria — and above all — I gave orders that they should not remain in the house. . . . Did I give orders, or didn't I? (*She approaches the others, who have crowded around the peasants.*) Take care! Do not touch them; they are all infected with diphtheria!

(*No one listens to her; she steps aside with dignity, remains standing motionless, and waits.*)

Petristcheff (*sniffing*). Diphtheria? don't know; but there is some infectious matter in the air. Don't you smell it?

Betsy. Don't talk! Wowó, in which bag?

Vassili Leoniditch. In that one, in that one. He is coming, he is coming closer.

Petristcheff. What is it now — spirit vapor or vapor spirit?

Betsy. Here your cigarettes come in just right for once. Smoke, do smoke, closer to me.

(PETRISTCHEFF *bends forward and smokes on her.*)

Vassili Leoniditch. He'll find it, I tell you. Eh?

Grossmann (*looks excitedly at the third peasant*). Here, here. I feel that it is here.

Fat Lady. Do you feel a twitching?

(GROSSMANN *bends down to the bag and draws out the spoon.*)

All. Bravo! (*General enthusiasm.*)

Vassili Leoniditch. Ah! do you see where our teaspoon's been? (*To the peasant.*) That's the kind you are?

Third Peasant. What kind am I? I did not take your spoon. What is he about? I have taken nothing, I have taken nothing, my conscience is clear. And he could do anything! I saw at once it wasn't anything good he wanted. Hand me your bag, said he. I have taken nothing, Christ is my witness,* I have taken nothing.

(*The young people encircle him and laugh.*)

* At these words the Russian peasant crosses himself.

Leonid Fedorovitch (*angry at his son*). Always and forever your foolish tricks! (*To the third peasant.*) Calm yourself, good man. We know that you have not taken anything. It was an experiment.

Grossmann (*takes off his bandage and acts as if he were coming to*). Water, if I may ask . . . Have the goodness.

(*Every one is busy about him.*)

Vassili Leoniditch. Let us go to the coachmen's room. I will show you what a hound I have there. *Épatant!* Eh?

Betsy. What an ugly word. Don't we say dog?

Vassili Leoniditch. No, that won't do. I surely cannot say of you: What an *épatant* PERSON is Betsy! I must say: GIRL. So it is here, too. Eh? Maria Konstantinovna, am I not right? Well said? (*He laughs.*)

Maria Konstantinovna. Let us go.

(*Exeunt* MARIA KONSTANTINOVNA, BETSY, PETRIST-CHEFF, *and* VASSILI LEONIDITCH.)

Scene XVIII.

The Same except Betsy, Maria Konstantinovna, Petristcheff, *and* Vassili Leoniditch.

Fat Lady (to Grossmann). What? How? Have you recovered? (*Grossmann does not answer. To Sachatoff.*) Sergei Ivanovitch, did you not feel a twitching?

Sachatoff. I didn't feel anything whatever. But it was fine, it was fine. A perfect success.

Baroness. Admirable! Ça ne le fait pas souffrir?

Leonid Fedorovitch. Pas le moins du monde.

Professor (to Grossmann). Will you permit me? (*He hands a thermometer to the physician.*) At the beginning of the experiment it was 99. (*To the physician.*) Wasn't it so? Have the kindness to take his pulse. A loss is inevitable.

Physician (to Grossmann). Well, Sir, will you let me feel your pulse? Let us examine, let us examine. (*He takes out his watch and grasps his hand.*)

Fat Lady (to Grossmann). Pardon me. But the condition in which you have been cannot be called sleep?

Grossmann (tired). A kind of hypnosis.

Sachatoff. We are to understand then that you have hypnotized yourself?

Grossmann. And why not? Hypnosis arises not alone from association, from the sounding of a tomtom, as for instance in the experiments of Charcot, but from the mere entrance into the hypnotic zone.

Sachatoff. Let us assume that it is so; still it remains desirable to have a more exact definition of what hypnosis is.

Professor. Hypnosis is the phenomenon of the conversion of one force into another.

Grossmann. Charcot defines it differently.

Sachatoff. Pardon me, pardon me. That is your definition; but Liebault has himself told me . . .

Physician (letting go the pulse). Very well, and now the temperature.

Fat Lady (obtruding herself). No, pardon me! I agree with Alexei Vladimirovitch. I will give you the best proof. When after my illness I lay unconscious, I was seized by a longing to speak. I am in general reticent; but then I was seized by a longing to speak and to speak, and I spoke, said the people, so that all were astonished. (*To Sachatoff.*) However, I believe I have interrupted you?

Sachatoff (dignified). Not in the least. Tut, tut.

Physician. Pulse 82, temperature has risen half a degree.

Professor. There is the proof. So it had to be, too. (*He takes out a note book and writes.*) 82, correct? And 99½? The approach of hypnosis is unfailingly followed by an increased action of the heart.

Physician. I can testify as a physician that your prediction has come perfectly true.

Professor (to Sachatoff). Your opinion then?

Sachatoff. I was about to say that Liebault told me hypnosis is only a special mental state of greater impressibility.

Professor. To be sure. But the main thing is still the law of equivalence.

Grossmann. Besides, Liebault is far from being an authority; but Charcot has instituted the most varied investigations, and demonstrated that hypnosis is induced by a stroke, a trauma.

Sachatoff. I do not at all deny Charcot's labors. I know him, too; I only say what Liebault told me. . . .

Grossmann (excited). There are three thousand sick in the Salpetrière, and I have taken a whole course there.

Professor. Pardon me, gentlemen. That is not the point at issue.

Together.

Fat Lady (obtruding herself). I will make it plain to you in two words. When my husband was ill, all the physicians gave him up. . . .

Leonid Fedorovitch. But let us go into the house. Dear Baroness, if you please.

(*They go away, all talking together, one interrupting the other.*)

SCENE XIX.

The three peasants, the COOK, FEDOR IVANITCH, TANIA, *the* OLD COOK (*on the stove*), LEONID FEDOROVITCH, *and* HER LADYSHIP.

Her Ladyship (holding Leonid Fedorovitch back by the sleeve). How often have I begged of you to make no arrangements in the house. You know nothing but your nonsense. And I must take the responsibility. They will infect everybody.

Leonid Fedorovitch. Who? What? I don't understand a word.

Her Ladyship. How? People who are afflicted with diphtheria pass the night in the kitchen, which is related to the house in a thousand ways.

Leonid Fedorovitch. But I . . .

Her Ladyship. What I?

Leonid Fedorovitch.   I know of nothing whatever.

Her Ladyship.   But you should know if you
wish to be the head of the family.   One does
not do such things.

Leonid Fedorovitch.   I had no idea . . . I
thought . . .

Her Ladyship.   Exasperating to listen to you!

(LEONID FEDOROVITCH *remains silent.*)

Her Ladyship (*to Fedor Ivanitch*).   Away
with them at once!   I do not want to see them
in my kitchen!   It is terrible, nobody obeys,
all to spite me . . .!   I send them away from
one place; they let them in again at another.
(*She talks herself more and more into a rage and
begins to cry.*)   All to spite me!   All to spite
me!   And in my illness!   Doctor! doctor!
Peter Petrovitch! . . . He, too, is away!

(*Exit, sobbing.*   LEONID FEDOROVITCH *follows her.*)

SCENE XX.

The three peasants, TANIA, FEDOR IVANITCH, *the* COOK,
and the OLD COOK (*on the stove*).

Tableaux.   All remain standing silent for some time.

Third Peasant.   Heaven rest their souls.
A little more and they would hand one over to

the police. In my whole life I have not had anything to do with the courts. Let's go to a lodging-house, children.

Fedor Ivanitch (to Tania). What's to be done now?

Tania. Only keep cool, Fedor Ivanitch. Into the coachmen's room with them.

Fedor Ivanitch. Into the coachmen's room? That is impossible! The coachman has already complained that it is crowded with dogs.

Tania. Into the domestics' room then.

Fedor Ivanitch. And if it's found out?

Tania. Nobody will find it out. Don't fear, Fedor Ivanitch. Can we send them away in the middle of the night? They wouldn't find their way.

Fedor Ivanitch. Well, do what you please; only see that they don't remain here. (*Exit.*)

SCENE XXI.

The three peasants, TANIA, the COOK, and the OLD COOK. The peasants pick up their bags.

Old Cook. Look, such damnèd vermin! It goes too well with them! Vermin!

Cook. Hush, you at least! You ought to thank God that they did not see you.

Tania.   Come along then, little uncles, into the domestics' room.

First Peasant.   Well, and our business? How is it, so to speak, with the signature? How, can we hope?

Tania   In an hour we shall know all.

Second Peasant.   Will you be sly enough?

Tania (laughs).   So God will.

(*Curtain falls.*)

ACT III.

The action takes place in the evening of the same day, in the small reception room where LEONID FEDORO-VITCH *usually makes his experiments.*

●

SCENE I.

LEONID FEDOROVITCH *and the* PROFESSOR.

Leonid Fedorovitch. What do you think, shall we risk the *séance* with our new medium?

Professor. Certainly. The medium is undoubtedly strong. But above all it is desirable that our mediumistic *séance* should take place to-day, and moreover with the same persons. Undoubtedly, the influence of the mediumistic force must manifest itself in Grossmann; then the connection and unity of the phenomena will be still plainer. You will convince yourself, if the medium shall be as powerful as before, that Grossmann will get into a vibrating motion.

Leonid Fedorovitch. Then I will call Semion and invite the company.

Professor. Yes, yes. I only want to make a few notes.

(*He takes out a note book and writes.*)

SCENE II.

The Same and SACHATOFF.

Sachatoff. • In there, in Anna Pavlovna's room, they are sitting at the card table. I as the man of straw . . . and besides as a curious spectator, announce myself to you. . . . Well, will the *séance* take place?

Leonid Fedorovitch. Certainly, it will undoubtedly take place.

Sachatoff. What, without the mediumistic force of Mr. Kaptchitch?

Leonid Fedorovitch. *Vous avez la main heureuse.* Just think, the same peasant of whom I told you proved himself to be an unquestionable medium.

Sachatoff. Remarkable! Oh, that is exceedingly interesting.

Leonid Fedorovitch. Yes, yes. We put him to a little experimental test after tea.

Sachatoff. Did it succeed, and are you convinced?

Leonid Fedorovitch. Thoroughly, he proved himself a medium of unusual force.

Sachatoff (*incredulous*). Remarkable!

Leonid Fedorovitch. It turned out that in the domestics' room it had already been long noticed. He sits down to a plate, and the spoon hops as of itself into his hand. (*To the Professor.*) Do you hear that?

Professor. No, *that* I have not heard.

Sachatoff (*to the Professor*). But you surely admit the possibility of such phenomena?

Professor. What phenomena?

Sachatoff. Well, in general, Spiritualistic, mediumistic, and, in short, supernatural phenomena.

Professor. The question is: what do we call supernatural? When — not a living being, man, but a piece of stone attracted a nail to itself, how did research regard this phenomenon: as natural or supernatural?

Sachatoff. Yes, very true; but such phenomena as the attraction of a magnet constantly repeat themselves.

Professor. It is just so here. The phenomenon repeats itself, and we seek to investigate it. More: we seek to range the investigated phenomena under the laws common to all other

phenomena.   The phenomena, surely, appear
as supernatural only because we ascribe the
causes of the phenomena to the medium itself.
But that is false.   The phenomena are not produced by the medium, but by a spiritual force
acting through the medium, and that is a great
difference.   The solution of the question lies
— in the law of equivalence.

Sachatoff.   Yes, very true, but . . .

Scene III.

The Same and Tania (*enters and gets behind the por-
tière*).

Leonid Fedorovitch.   But you must know one
thing.   As in the case of Home and Kaptchitch,
so also in the case of this medium, we must not
rely on anything in advance.   It may fail, but
it may just as likely prove a complete materialization.

Sachatoff.   A materialization even ?   In what
is this materialization to consist ?

Leonid Fedorovitch.   In the apparition of a
deceased person, your father, your grandfather;
in that he takes you by the hand, gives you
something ; or in that somebody suddenly rises
in the air, as happened to Alexei Vladimirovitch
at our last *séance.*

Professor. True, true. But the principal thing is: the explanation of the phenomena and their classification under the general laws.

Scene IV.

The Same and the Fat Lady.

Fat Lady. Anna Pavlovna hàs permitted me to come over to you.

Leonid Fedorovitch. Pleased to have you.

Fat Lady. But how it fatigued Grossmann! He could scarcely hold the cup. Did you notice how pale he grew (*to the Professor*) the moment he drew near? I observed it at once, and first told Anna Pavlovna about it.

Professor. Without doubt the loss of vital force.

Fat Lady. I say too that it must not be done to excess. Just think of it, the hypnotizer suggested to an acquaintance of mine, Vieratchka Konchina — you know her — that she should stop smoking; then her back began to ache.

Professor (*trying to speak.*) The height of the temperature and the pulse plainly point to . . .

Fat Lady. Allow me one moment. I tell

her : it is much better to smoke than to suffer so from the nerves.   Of course, smoking is harmful, and I too would much rather give it up ; but what do you want, it won't do. . . . I didn't smoke once for two weeks, then I couldn't stand it any longer.

Professor (again tries to speak).   Plainly point to. . .

Fat Lady.   But no, allow me.   Only two words.   You say : a loss of forces ?   And I wanted to say, when I rode in the stage . . . The roads were abominable at that time, you cannot remember the time, and I have made the observation, you may say what you please, that our nervousness comes only from the railroads.   I, for instance, cannot sleep while travelling.— You might kill me, but I couldn't go .to sleep.

Professor (wants to begin again, but the Fat Lady will not let him).   The loss of force . . .

Sachatoff (smiling).   Yes, yes.

(LEONID FEDOROVITCH *rings the bell.*)

Fat Lady.   I do not close an eye for one, two, three nights, and in spite of that I can't go to sleep.

SCENE V.

The Same and GREGORI.

Leonid Fedorovitch. Tell Fedor, please, that he is to prepare everything for the *séance*, and call Semion here; Semion, the boy, you understand?

Gregori. At your service! (*Exit.*)

SCENE VI.

LEONID FEDOROVITCH, *the* PROFESSOR, *the* FAT LADY, *and* TANIA (*hidden*).

Professor (*to Sachatoff*). The height of the temperature and the pulse have pointed to a loss of vital force. It will be exactly so in the mediumistic phenomena. The law of the conservation of force . . .

Fat Lady. Yes, yes. I only wanted to say besides how pleased I am that a simple peasant has proven himself a medium. That is wonderful; I have always said the Slavophiles . . .

Leonid Fedorovitch. Let us go into the front room meanwhile.

Fat Lady. Permit me to say two words : . . . The Slavophiles are right; but I have always

told my husband such a thing must not be carried to excess.   Always the golden mean.   How
can any one maintain that with the people
everything was good when I have seen with my
own eyes . . .

Leonid Fedorovitch.   Will you not please go
into the front room ?.

Fat Lady.   Such a scapegrace, and drinks
already.   I gave him a good scolding on the
spot ; he was thankful to me later on.   They
are — like children, and children need — I have
always said so — love *and* severity.

(All exeunt talking.)

Scene VII.

TANIA (*alone, comes from her hiding place behind the
door*).

Tania.   O, if it would only succeed !   (*She
fastens threads.*)

Scene VIII.

TANIA *and* BETSY (*entering hastily*).

Betsy.   Papa not here ?   (*Looking at Tania.*)
What are you doing here ?

Tania.   I, Lisaveta Leonidovna, I only happened to pass, I wanted to . . . I came in . . . (*Embarrassed.*)

Betsy. Is not the *séance* to take place here soon? (*She observes that Tania draws in the threads, fixes her eyes upon her, and suddenly bursts out laughing loudly.*) Tania! So you do everything? Now don't deny it any more; the last time it was you, too? You, you?

Tania. Lisaveta Leonidovna, sweet, dear lady!

Betsy (*charmed*). O, that is excellent! I should not have believed it! But why do you do that?

Tania. Dear gracious lady, do not betray me!

Betsy. Surely not, not for the world! It gives me a mad pleasure! But *how* do you do it?

Tania. This is the way; I hide, and, when the light is out, I steal out and do everything.

Betsy (*pointing to a thread*). And what is this for? Hold, don't tell me, I know it already, you pull . . .

Tania. Lisaveta Leonidovna, sweet, dear lady, I want to be quite frank with you. Until now I have only been doing it for fun, but to-day I have an important matter in mind.

Betsy.   How? What? An important matter?

Tania.   You know, of course, peasants have come who want to buy land, and your papa don't want to sell to them, and has not signed the document and has returned it to them. Fedor Ivanitch says : the spirits forbade him. So the thought came to me.

Betsy.   But you are a sly thing! Only go ahead, go ahead.   But how are you going to do it ?   .

Tania.   I have planned it so : when they put out the light, at once I begin to rap, to throw things, to work about their heads with the thread, and at the close the document comes down from above,— I have it with me,—and I let it fall on the table.

Betsy.   And what's to happen then ?

Tania.   What's to happen then ?   All will be astonished ; for did not the peasants have the document, and suddenly it is here.   Now I command . . .

Betsy.   But Semion is the medium to-day !

Tania.   I command him then . . . (*She cannot speak for laughing.*)   I command him then to choke whoever happens to be in his reach. Only not your papa — he will not dare do that — the rest he may choke until it is signed.

Betsy (*laughs*).   But that is not the way it is done; the medium himself does nothing.

Tania.   That's all the same; perhaps it will succeed so, too.

SCENE IX.

TANIA *and* FEDOR IVANITCH.   BETSY *makes a sign to* TANIA, *and goes away.*

Fedor Ivanitch.   What are you doing here?

Tania.   I have come to you, dear Fedor Ivanitch.

Fedor Ivanitch.   What do you want?

Tania.   I have come on account of that affair of mine about which I asked you.

Fedor Ivanitch.   Your suit is accepted, they gave their consent.   Only it has not yet been wet.

Tania (*squeals*).   Is that really true?

Fedor Ivanitch.   If I tell you so.   He says: I will consult with my old woman, and then as God wills.

Tania.   Did he say that?   (*She squeals.*) Ah, dearest, best Fedor Ivanitch, my whole life long will I pray for you.

Fedor Ivanitch.   Tut, tut, tut!   There's no time for that now.   I must get things in order for the *séance.*

Tania. I will help you. What is to be got in order?

Fedor Ivanitch. What? — Here, the table — into the middle of the room, chairs, the guitar, the harmonica. The lamp is not needed — candles.

Tania (assisting Fedor Ivanitch). So then. Here the guitar, and the inkstand here. (*Puts it down.*) So?

Fedor Ivanitch. But do they really want to have Semion here?

Tania. I suppose it must be so. For they have had him here before.

Fedor Ivanitch. Amazing! (*He puts on his eyeglasses.*) But is he clean?

Tania. How am I to know that?

Fedor Ivanitch. Do you know . . .

Tania. What, Fedor Ivanitch?

Fedor Ivanitch. Go get the nail brush and some toilet soap; you may get it from my room — cut off his claws and wash him very nicely.

Tania. He will wash himself.

Fedor Ivanitch. Tell him at least, and ask him also to put on clean linen.

Tania. Very well, Fedor Ivanitch. (*Exit.*)

Scene X.

Fedor Ivanitch *alone, takes a chair.*

Fedor Ivanitch.   Cultured, they are very cultured, Alexei Vladimirovitch, for instance. He
is a professor, yet I must constantly doubt him.
The superstition among the people, vulgar
superstition, is combated, the belief in hob-
goblins, magicians, witches . . . And yet, if
one searches more closely, it is the same· superstition.   For can it be possible that the
souls of the deceased should talk, play on the
guitar? Either they deceive one another or
they deceive themselves. The story about
Semion also is hard for me to swallow. (*He looks
at the album.*)   And here is their Spiritualistic
album, too.   Is it possible, I ask, to photograph
a spirit?   What a picture! —a Turk and Leonid Fedorovitch together.   Strange weakness
of man !

Scene XI.

Fedor Ivanitch *and* Leonid Fedorovitch.

Leonid Fedorovitch (*entering*).   Well, ready?
Fedor Ivanitch (*rising slowly*).   Ready. (*Smiling.*)   I only don't know whether your new me-

dium won't compromise you, Leonid Fedorovitch.

Leonid Fedorovitch. O no, Alexei Vladimirovitch and myself have already experimented
with him. An extraordinarily powerful medium !

Fedor Ivanitch. I don't understand that, of
course. But is he clean ? You have surely
not thought of asking him to wash his hands,
and that surely won't do.

Leonid Fedorovitch. His hands ? Ah, yes.
Do you think they are not clean, Fedor Ivanitch ?

Fedor Ivanitch. Of course, a peasant. And
there will be ladies here, also Maria Vassilievna.

Leonid Fedorovitch. Very well.

Fedor Ivanitch. I wanted to tell you besides : Timofei, the coachman, was here, and
complained that on account of the dogs he simply didn't know how to steer clear of all the
filth.

*Leonid Fedorovitch (placing the things on the
table in order, absent-minded).* What dogs ?

Fedor Ivanitch. Three greyhounds were sent
to-day to Vassili Leoniditch ; these have been
taken to the coachmen's room.

Leonid Fedorovitch (vexed). Tell Anna

Pavlovna; whatever she may order done; I have no time.

Fedor Ivanitch. But you know her passion . . .

Leonid Fedorovitch. Let her do what she pleases. The boy gives me no end of annoyance . . . and I have no time.

SCENE XII.

The Same and SEMION (*in a sleeveless jacket, enters and smiles*).

Semion. It is your lordship's will?

Leonid Fedorovitch. Yes, yes. Show your hands. Well, very well. Now do as before, my son; sit down and abandon yourself to your feelings. And think of nothing whatever.

Semion. What should I think? The more one thinks, the worse.

Leonid Fedorovitch. Exactly, exactly. The weaker consciousness, the greater the force. Do not think, and abandon yourself to your mood. Do you feel like sleeping — sleep; do you feel like walking — walk; do you understand?

Semion. What is there to understand here? That doesn't take much shrewdness.

Leonid Fedorovitch.   The main point is — do not get confused.   You might yourself be easily astonished.   You must know just as we live, so there lives close to us a never-seen world of spirits.

Fedor Ivanitch (*improving*).   Invisible beings, do you understand ?

Semion (*laughs*).   What is there to understand here ?   As you say that, the thing is very simple.

Leonid Fedorovitch.   You might rise into the air or something else, only do not be afraid.

Semion.   Why should I be afraid ?   That won't hurt.

Leonid Fedorovitch.   Very well then, I shall go and call the company.   Is everything ready?

Fedor Ivanitch.   I think everything is ready.

Leonid Fedorovitch.   And the slates ?

Fedor Ivanitch.   Are downstairs, I shall get them at once.   (*Exit.*)

SCENE XIII.

LEONID FEDOROVITCH *and* SEMION.

Leonid Fedorovitch.   Well, that's right.   Do not get confused, and move freely.

Semion.   Take off the jacket, perhaps.   Then I can move more freely.

Leonid Fedorovitch. The jacket? No, no, that is not necessary. (*Exit.*)

Scene XIV.

Semion alone.

Semion. Again she bids me do all that, and she will again throw her things. Indeed, she isn't afraid!

Scene XV.

Semion *and* Tania (*enters, in her stockings, her dress of the color of the wall paper.* Semion *laughs*).

Tania (*hisses*). 'Sh! 'sh! . . . They might hear! Paste these matches on your fingers as before (*he fastens them*). Now, do you still know all?

Semion (*bends the fingers in*). The very first, wet the matches. Flourish them in the air — one. Two — chatter with the teeth, so . . . Number three I have forgotten.

Tania. And three is the most important point. Do not forget: when the paper falls on the table — I will besides ring the bell — instantly you do so with your arms — wider apart, and seize. You seize any one who sits near. And when you have seized one, you squeeze (*laughs*), whether lady or gentleman. You have only one thing to do — to squeeze and to squeeze and not to let go, as if you were in sleep, and gnash your teeth or bellow, look, so . . . (*she bellows*). And when I play on the guitar, then you act as if you were about to wake up, stretch yourself, you know, so. Then you awake. . . . Do you know all?

Semion. I know all ; but it is awfully laughable.

Tania. But you must not laugh. Should you laugh once, however, that will not dish the matter. They will think it was in sleep. But remember only not to sleep in reality when they put out the light.

Semion. Don't fear, I'll pinch my ears.

Tania. Now be wide awake, Semotchka, my sweetheart. Only do everything, and be not afraid. He must sign, you will see. They are coming. (*She creeps under the sofa.*)

Scene XVI.

Semion *and* Tania. *There enter:* Grossmann, *the* Professor, Leonid Fedorovitch, *the* Fat Lady, *the* Physician, Sachatoff, *and* Her Ladyship. Semion *is standing by the door.*

Leonid Fedorovitch. All unbelievers are solemnly invited! Although our medium is new, and here only by accident, nonetheless I look for very remarkable manifestations to-day.

Sachatoff. Interesting, most interesting.

Fat Lady (pointing to Semion). Mais il est très-bien.

Her Ladyship. Great heavens, a kitchen boy, yes, but . . .

Sachatoff. Women never believe in what their husbands do. They do not even recognize it!

Her Ladyship. Of course not. In Kaptchitch, I admit, there is something special; but God knows what this is!

Fat Lady. No, no, pardon me, Anna Pavlovna, that is not to be solved so simply. When I was still a girl, I had a remarkable dream. You know there are dreams of which one does not know when they begin, when they end, and such a dream I had . . .

Scene XVII.

The Same. Vassili Leoniditch *and* Petristcheff *enter.*

Fat Lady. And through this dream much was revealed unto me. Now-a-days these young people (*she points to Petristcheff and Vassili Leoniditch*) deny just everything.

Vassili Leoniditch. By no means, I assure you I deny nothing. Eh?

Scene XVIII.

The Same. Betsy *and* Maria Konstantinovna *enter, and begin a conversation with* Petristcheff.

Fat Lady. How can we deny the supernatural? They say it is incompatible with human reason. But reason may be dull, how is it then? Did we not have spirit manifestations every evening on Garden Street? You have surely heard about it? The son of my aunt — what do we say now for cousin? ... I always forget these new expressions — he went there three nights in succession, and did not see anything anyway, therefore I say . . .

Leonid Fedorovitch. Who of the company will remain here?

Fat Lady. I, I!

Sachatoff. I !

Her Ladyship (*to the physician*). Will you really remain here ?

Physician. Yes, one must at least for once see what it is that Alexei Vladimirovitch finds in the matter. To deny without disproof won't do either.

Her Ladyship. The treatment is then by all means to be resumed this evening ?

Physician. What is to be resumed ? Ah, yes, resume taking the powders. Yes, just take them. Yes, yes, just take them. I will also come.

Her Ladyship. Please. (*Loud.*) When you are through, *messieurs et mesdames*, I invite you to my room in order to recover yourselves from the emotion ; we can also finish our game.

Fat Lady. Certainly.

Sachatoff. Yes, yes !

(*Exit* HER LADYSHIP.)

SCENE XIX.

The Same except HER LADYSHIP.

Betsy (*to Petristcheff*). I tell you, stay! I promise you something extraordinary. Will you wager with me ?

Maria Konstantinovna. Do you believe in it then ?

Betsy. To-day I believe.

Maria Konstantinovna (to Petristcheff). And do you believe ?

Petristcheff. Never, never will I trust in alluring promises. Very well, if Elisaveta Leonidovna commands.

Vassili Leoniditch. Let us stay, Maria Konstantinovna. Eh ? I want to get off something, *épatant.*

Maria Konstantinovna. Look out, you must not make me laugh. You know very well I cannot suppress it.

Vassili Leoniditch (loud). I — stay !

Leonid Fedorovitch (severe). I request the ladies and gentlemen who stay here not to turn this matter into ridicule. It is of a very serious nature.

Petristcheff. Do you hear ? Well then, we will stay. Wowó, sit here, but look out you don't get frightened.

Betsy. Yes, you laugh, and you will see what will happen.

Vassili Leoniditch. And if it does really happen ! It might become serious ! Eh ?

Petristcheff (trembles). Oo, oo, how fright-

ened I am. Maria Konstantinovna, I am afraid.
... My teet fremble!

Betsy (laughs). Be quiet!

(*All sit down.*)

Leonid Fedorovitch. Sit down, sit down,
gentlemen. Sit down, Semion!

Semion. At your service! (*Sits down on
the edge of the chair.*)

Leonid Fedorovitch. Sit properly.

Professor. Sit exactly in the middle of the
chair, entirely unconstrained. (*He seats Semion
properly.*)

(BETSY, MARIA KONSTANTINOVNA, *and* VASSILI LEONI-
DITCH *laugh.*)

Leonid Fedorovitch (with raised voice). I request the ladies and gentlemen who remain
here not to jest, and to take the matter se-
riously. It might have unfortunate conse-
quences. Wowó, do you hear? If you cannot
sit still, go away!

Vassili Leoniditch. Peace! (*He hides behind
the back of the Fat Lady.*)

Leonid Fedorovitch. Alexei Vladimirovitch,
put him to sleep.

Professor. No, why should I, when Anton
Barissovitch is present? He is vastly more ex-

perienced in this matter and possesses a greater force.　Anton Barissovitch !

Grossmann.　Ladies and gentlemen !　I am not really a Spiritualist.　I have only studied Hypnotism.　To be sure, I have studied Hypnotism in all its known forms.　But I am entirely ignorant of what is described as Spiritualism.　From the falling asleep of the subject, I may expect the hypnotic phenomena known to me : lethargy, abulie, anæsthesie, analgie, catalepsy, and suggestions of the most varied kind. But it is not these phenomena that are presented to our study here, but others, and therefore it would be desirable to know in advance the nature of the anticipated phenomena, and what scientific importance they claim.

Sachatoff.　I fully agree with the views expressed by Mr. Grossmann.　Such an explanation would be very, very interesting.

Leonid Fedorovitch (to the Professor).　I trust, Alexei Vladimirovitch, you will gladly give us a short explanation.

Professor.　Cheerfully ; if it is desired, I am willing to give the explanation.　(*To the physician.*)　And you will have the goodness to take the temperature and the pulse.　My explanation will be necessarily cursory and brief.

Leonid Fedorovitch. Yes, brief, brief . . .

Physician. Directly! (*He takes out the ther-mometer and hands it over.*) Well, noble youth! . . . (*Puts thermometer in his mouth.*)

Semion. At your service!

Professor (*rises, turns towards the Fat Lady, and then sits down*). Ladies and gentlemen! The phenomenon that we are to study is usually represented by the one party as something new, by the other as something transcending natural relations. Neither the one nor the other is justified. This phenomenon is not new, but as old as the world; nor is it supernatural, it is on the contrary subject to the same eternal laws which all created things obey. This phenomenon is usually defined as the communion with the spirit world. This definition is not exact. According to this definition the spirit world is opposed to the world of phenomena, but without any justification. There is no such antithesis. There is such a close contact between the two worlds that it is quite impossible to draw the boundary line that, separates the one from the other. We say: matter is composed of molecules . . .

Petristcheff. Tiresome matter!

(*Whispering, laughing.*)

Professor (*stops, then continues*). The molecules — of atoms, but the atoms have no exten-
sion and are essentially nothing else than cen-
tres of force. That is, to express it more precisely, not force, but energy — the energy
which is something just as specific and inde-
.structible as matter. But as there is only one
matter, however varied its forms, so also with
energy. Until very recently we knew of but
four forms of energy, each of which was con-
vertible into the other. We knew of dynamical, thermal, electrical, and chemical energy.
But the four forms of energy do not by any
means comprise the entire multiplicity of its
manifestations. The manifestations of energy
are multiform, and it is one of these new but
little known forms of energy which we are to
study. I refer to the energy of mediumism.

(*Again whispering and laughing from the corner where
the young people are sitting.*)

Professor (*stops, looks around severely, and
continues*). Reports of mediumistic energy
come down to mankind from ancient times.
Prophecies, forebodings, visions, and many
other phenomena are — nothing but manifestations of mediumistic energy. The phenomena

it produces are known from antiquity. But the energy itself was not recognized as such until recent times, so long as the sphere was not recognized whose undulations cause the mediumistic phenomena. As the phenomena of light were inexplicable so long as the presence of an imponderable substance, ether, was not recognized, so also the mediumistic phenomena remained a mystery to us before the now indisputable truth was established that there is a still finer imponderable substance between the particles of the ether which is not subject to the law of the three dimensions. . . .

(Again whispering, laughing, and squeaking.)

Professor (again looks around severely). And as the mathematical calculations have indisputably demonstrated the existence of an imponderable ether which produces the phenomena of light and electricity, just so a brilliant series of the most reliable experiments by the gifted Herrmann, Schmidt, and Joseph Schmatzhofen have unquestionably demonstrated the reality of a substance which fills the universe and may be described as the spiritual ether.

Fat Lady. Yes, now it is clear to me. How grateful . . .

Leonid Fedorovitch.   Yes ; but is it not possible, Alexei Vladimirovitch, to express yourself . . . a little more briefly ?

Professor (without replying).   Thus the laws
of the mediumistic phenomena have been set
forth by a series of strictly scientific experiments and investigations, as I have had the
honor to explain to you.   These experiments
have taught us that the entrance of certain persons into the hypnotic condition, which differs
from common sleep only in this, that in the
entrance into this sleep physiological action is
not only not lowered, but increased, as we have
seen above — it was established, I say, that the
entrance of any subject into this condition necessarily produces certain disturbances in the
spiritual ether,— disturbances which perfectly
resemble those produced by the immersion of a
hard substance in a fluid.   Now these disturbances are what we call mediumistic phenomena. . . .

(*Laughing, whispering.*)

Sachatoff.   That is perfectly correct and
plain.   But allow me one question : if, as you
are pleased to say, the going to sleep of the
medium produces disturbances of the spiritual
ether, why is it that these disturbances, as is

usually assumed at Spiritualistic *séances*, always take the shape of manifestations of deceased persons?

Professor. That is because the particles of this spiritual ether are nothing but the souls of the living, the dead, and the unborn, so that every agitation of this spiritual ether necessarily produces the familiar movement of its particles. But these particles are nothing else than the souls of men, which enter into communion with one another in consequence of this movement.

Fat Lady (to Sachatoff). What is the difficulty in comprehending this? It is very simple . . . I thank you, I thank you very much!

Leonid Fedorovitch. Now, I think, everything is plain, and we can begin.

Physician. The young fellow is in a perfectly normal state. Temperature 99, pulse 74.

Professor (takes out his note book and writes). In confirmation of what I have just had the honor to explain I may cite the circumstance that the falling asleep of the medium will undoubtedly be accompanied by a rise of the temperature and of the pulse, just as in cases of hypnotism.

Leonid Fedorovitch. Yes, yes, pardon me, please, I was only going to answer the question of Sergei Ivanovitch: how we know that the souls of the deceased enter into communication with us. We know it by the fact that the spirit which appears tells us forthwith — quite simply as I now tell this — tells us forthwith who he is, and why he has come, and where he is staying, and whether all is well with him. At our last *séance* the Spaniard Don Castilios appeared and told us everything. He told us who he was, when he died, that he was suffering tortures because he had taken part in the Inquisition. Still more, he told us what was happening to him at the very hour when he was speaking to us, and, strange to say, he was to be born again for the earth at the very hour when he was speaking with us, and therefore was obliged to cut short the conversation begun with us. But you shall really see with your own eyes . . .

Fat Lady (interrupting). Ah, how interesting! Perhaps the Spaniard was born in our house and is now a child.

Leonid Fedorovitch. Quite possible!

Professor. I think it is time to begin.

Leonid Fedorovitch. I was only going to say . . .

Professor. It is already late.

Leonid Fedorovitch. Very well, then. Let

us begin. Anton Barissovitch, will you have the goodness to put the medium to sleep?

Grossmann. How do you want me to put the subject to sleep? There are four different ways in use, Braid's method, the Egyptian symbol, the method of Charcot.

Leonid Fedorovitch (to the Professor). That is quite immaterial, I think.

Professor. There is no difference.

Grossmann. Then I will apply my method which I demonstrated at Odessa.

Leonid Fedorovitch. If you please!

(GROSSMANN *makes passes over* SEMION'S *head.—*SE-MION *closes his eyes and stretches himself.*)

Grossmann (observing). He is falling asleep, he is asleep. A strikingly sudden appearance of hypnosis. The subject clearly is already in the anæsthetic condition. A remarkable, an extraordinarily impressionable subject; one might make interesting experiments with him! ... (*He sits down, rises, and sits down again.*) Now one might pierce his hand. If you wish ...

Professor (to Leonid Fedorovitch). Do you notice how the sleep of the medium is affecting Grossmann? He is beginning to vibrate ...

Leonid Fedorovitch. Yes, yes. Can we put out the light now?

Sachatoff. But what is the use of darkness?

Professor. Darkness? Darkness is one of the conditions under which the mediumistic energy manifests itself, just as a definite temperature is the condition of certain manifestations of chemical or dynamical energy.

Leonid Fedorovitch. Not always. To many, among them myself also, they have appeared in light, in broad daylight even.

Professor (interrupting). Is the light to be put out?

Leonid Fedorovitch. Yes, yes. (*Puts out the lights.*) Ladies and gentlemen, I now bespeak your attention.

(TANIA *creeps from under the sofa and reaches out for the thread which she has fastened to the candlestick.*)

Petristcheff. Well, how I was amused by the Spaniard! How in the middle of the conversation — *piquer une tête,* as they say — he . . .

Betsy. Just wait and see what will happen.

Petristcheff. I fear only one thing — that Wowó might break out.

Vassili Leoniditch. Shall I? I'll fire off . . .

Leonid Fedorovitch. Gentlemen, please not to talk!

(*Quiet.*— SEMION *licks a finger, passes it over his knuckles, and saws the air.*)

Leonid Fedorovitch. It flashes! Do you see how it flashes!

Sachatoff. It flashes! Yes, yes, I see; but permit me . . .

Fat Lady. Where? where? Ah, I did not see it! There it is! Ah! . . .

Professor (whispers something to Leonid Fedorovitch and points to Grossmann, who is moving to and fro). Observe how he is vibrating. A double force!

(*Again flashing.*)

Leonid Fedorovitch (to the Professor). That is *he!*

Sachatoff. Who?

Leonid Fedorovitch. The Greek, Nicolas. That is his flashing. Is it not, Alexei Vladimirovitch?

Sachatoff. The Greek, Nicolas, who is he?

Professor. A Greek who was a monk at Byzantium in the time of Constantine, and who has often visited us of late.

Fat Lady. But where is he, where is he? I see nothing.

Leonid Fedorovitch. He is not to be seen either. Alexei Vladimirovitch, he is always particularly friendly towards you. Question him!

Professor (*in a peculiar voice*). Nicolas! Is that you?

(TANIA *raps twice against the wall.*)

Leonid Fedorovitch (*exultant*). It is he! It is he!

Fat Lady. Hu, hu! I'll go away!

Sachatoff. But why is it supposed that it is he?

Leonid Fedorovitch. It rapped twice. That is an affirmative answer; otherwise he would have kept silent.

(*Pause. Suppressed laughter in the young folks' corner.* TANIA *drops on the table a lamp-shade, a lead-pencil, and a pen-wiper.*)

Leonid Fedorovitch (*whispering*). Attention, gentlemen! A lamp-shade! Something else. A lead-pencil! Alexei Vladimirovitch, a lead-pencil!

Professor. Indeed, indeed! I am watching both him and Grossmann. Did you notice?

(GROSSMANN *rises and looks at the things that fell on the table.*)

Sachatoff. Pardon me, pardon me. I should like to convince myself if all this is not done by the medium himself.

Leonid Fedorovitch. Do you doubt? Sit down beside him then, and hold him fast by the hands. But you may be sure he is asleep.

Sachatoff (*wants to go; the thread which Tania lets down touches his head; he collapses terrified*). Y-ye-yes! Strange! Strange!

(*He goes farther, grasps* SEMION *by the elbow.* SEMION *bellows.*)

Professor (*to Leonid Fedorovitch*). Do you hear how Grossmann's proximity is affecting him? A new phenomenon, that must be noted. (*He runs out and makes a note, then he returns.*)

Leonid Fedorovitch. Yes ... but we must not leave Nicolas without response; we must begin ...

Grossmann (*rises, approaches Semion, lifts his hand, and lets it fall again*). Now it would be interesting to produce a contracture. The subject is in a state of complete hypnosis.

Professor (*to Leonid Fedorovitch*). You see? You see?

Grossmann. If you wish ...

Physician. . Please, dear friend, do not interfere with Alexei Vladimirovitch ... the thing is now getting serious.

Professor.   Let him.   He is already talking in his sleep.

Fat Lady.   How glad I am that I decided to stay here!   I am frightened, but nevertheless I am glad; for I have always told my husband, . . .

Leonid Fedorovitch.   I must request peace.

(TANIA *draws the thread over the head of the* FAT LADY.)

Fat Lady.   Oo!

Leonid Fedorovitch.   What is it?   What is it?

Fat Lady.   He took hold of my hair.

Leonid Fedorovitch (*whispering*).   Do not fear, give him your hand.   His hand is always cold ; but I like that.

Fat Lady (*hides her hands.*)   Not for anything in the world!

Sachatoff.   Yes, strange, strange!

Leonid Fedorovitch.   He is here, and desires to enter into communication with us.   Who would like to ask him a question?

Sachatoff.   Permit me to ask.

Professor.   Have the goodness.

Sachatoff.   Do I believe, or do I not believe?

(TANIA *raps twice.*)

Professor. An affirmative answer.

Sachatoff. Permit me to continue. Have I a ten-rouble note in my pocket?

(TANIA *raps many times and draws the thread over* SACHATOFF'S *head.*)

Sachatoff. Ah!... (*He seizes the thread and breaks it.*)

Professor. I should like to request those present not to put indefinite or jesting questions. It is disagreeable to him.

Sachatoff. No, pardon me, I have a thread in my hand.

Leonid Fedorovitch. A thread? Hold it fast. That happens frequently; not only cotton thread, but also silk cords of ancient times.

Sachatoff. Well, but where does this thread come from?

(TANIA *throws a pillow at him.*)

Sachatoff. Pardon me, pardon me, something soft has struck me on the head. Let us have a light — here something is passing ...

Professor. We must request you not to disturb the manifestations.

Fat Lady. For God's sake, do not make any disturbance. I should also like to put a question; may I?

Leonid Fedorovitch. Certainly, certainly! Just ask!

Fat Lady. I should like to consult him concerning my stomach. May one do that? I should like to ask what I am to take: aconite or belladonna?

(Pause. Whispering in the young folks' corner. Suddenly VASSILI LEONIDITCH *cries like an infant: ua, ua! Laughter. The young ladies and* PETRISTCHEFF *cover their mouths and noses and run away, breathing hard.*

Fat Lady. Ah! surely the monk has been born again?

Leonid Fedorovitch (in a rage, whispering in wrath). You think of nothing but your nonsense. If you cannot behave decently, then go away!

(*Exit* VASSILI LEONIDITCH.)

SCENE XX.

LEONID FEDOROVITCH, PROFESSOR, *the* FAT LADY, SACHATOFF, GROSSMANN, *the* PHYSICIAN, SEMION, *and* TANIA. (*Darkness. Pause.*)

Fat Lady. Ah, too bad! Now one cannot put any more questions. He is born.

Leonid Fedorovitch. By no means. That

was Wowó's nonsense. *He* is here. Just ask.

Professor. That happens frequently; jests and mockeries of this sort are quite usual. I presume *he* is still here. Besides, we can ask. Leonid Fedorovitch, will you?

Leonid Fedorovitch. No, please, you. I am in a bad humor. What an annoyance! Such a want of tact! . . .

Professor. Very well, then. Nicolas! Are you still here?

(TANIA *raps twice and knocks against the bell.* — SEMION *begins to bellow and saw the air with his hands. He seizes* SACHATOFF *and the* PROFESSOR, *and chokes them.*)

Professor. What an unexpected manifestation! A direct action upon the medium himself. That is unprecedented. Leonid Fedorovitch, will you take the observations; I don't feel well. He is choking me. Keep a strict watch on Grossmann! Now's the time to keep a bright lookout.

(TANIA *throws the document of the peasants on the table.*)

Leonid Fedorovitch. Something has fallen on the table.

Professor.   See what it is.

Leonid Fedorovitch.   A paper, a folded sheet of paper!

(TANIA *throws a traveller's inkstand.*)

Leonid Fedorovitch.   An inkstand!

(TANIA *throws a pen.*)

Leonid Fedorovitch.   A pen!

(SEMION *keeps on bellowing and choking.*)

Professor (*strangling*).   Pardon me, pardon me, an entirely new phenomenon, it is not the produced mediumistic energy, but the medium himself that is in action.   Do open the inkstand and place the pen on the paper; he wishes to write, he surely wishes to write.

(TANIA *steals up behind* LEONID FEDOROVITCH *and strikes him on the head with the guitar.*)

Leonid Fedorovitch.   He struck me on the head!   (*He looks on the table.*)   The pen does not yet write, and the paper is still folded together.

Professor.   See what the paper contains. Quick, quick.   Clearly the double force of him and Grossmann is causing disturbances.

Leonid Fedorovitch (*takes the paper out of the*

room and returns presently). Extraordinary! This paper is the contract with the peasants which İ refused to sign this morning and gave back to the peasants. It is likely *he* wants me to sign it.

Professor. Of course! Of course! Just ask him.

Leonid Fedorovitch. Nicolas! Do you wish . . .

        (TANIA *raps twice.*)

Professor. Do you hear? Evidently, evidently!

(LEONID FEDOROVITCH *takes the pen and leaves the room.*— TANIA *raps, plays on the guitar and the harmonica, and creeps back under the sofa.*— LEONID FEDOROVITCH *returns* — SEMION *stretches himself and expectorates.*)

Leonid Fedorovitch. He is waking up. We can light the candles.

Professor (*hastily*). Doctor, doctor, please, the temperature and the pulse. You will presently note a rise.

Leonid Fedorovitch (*lights the candles*). How now, incredulous ladies and gentlemen?

Physician (*approaches Semion and inserts the thermometer*). Well, noble youth! Slept well? Take this into your mouth, and give me your hand. (*Looks at his watch.*)

Sachatoff (draws up his shoulders). I can show that the medium cannot possibly have done all that has just passed here. But the thread? . . . I should only like to get an explanation of this thread.

Leonid Fedorovitch. The thread, the thread! But there have been much more important things.

Sachatoff. I don't know. At all events, *je réserve mon opinion*.

Fat Lady (to Sachatoff). By no means, how can you say: *je réserve mon opinion?* And the boy with the wings? Did you not see him? First I thought it was only a shimmer, but then it became clear, clear, as if in the flesh.

Sachatoff. I can only say what I saw. That I did not see, no.

Fat Lady. How is that possible? It was surely quite plainly to be seen. And from the left the monk in the black gown bent down to him . . .

Sachatoff (walks away). What an exaggeration!

Fat Lady (turning to the physician). You must have seen him. He rose by your side.

(The PHYSICIAN continues counting the pulse without listening to her.)

Fat Lady (to Grossmann). And a light, a light shone forth from him, especially about his face. And his features were so mild, so delicate, something super-earthly! (*She herself smiles softly.*)

Grossmann. I saw a phosphorescent light, I saw things moving about; but further than that I did not see anything.

Fat Lady (to Grossmann). But I beg of you! You say that so. That comes from your not believing in the future life, like all the *savants* of Charcot's school. But no one, no one in all the world can now take from me the belief in a future life.

(GROSSMANN *goes away from her.*)

Fat Lady. No, no, say what you will, that was one of the happiest hours of my life. When I heard Sarasate and this . . . Yes! (*No one listens to her. She goes to Semion.*) Well, *you* tell me, my son, what you felt. Did it torture you badly?

Semion (laughs). Certainly.

Fat Lady. But nevertheless it was endurable?

Semion. Certainly. (*To Leonid Fedorovitch.*) Shall I go now?

Leonid Fedorovitch. Go, go.

Physician (to the Professor). The pulse is as before; but the temperature has fallen.

Professor. Fallen? (*He thinks awhile and suddenly has it.*) So it had to be, too,—a fall had to take place! The two energies, inasmuch as they crossed each other, had to produce a kind of interference. Yes, yes.

Leonid Fedorovitch. I am only sorry for the one thing that we did not get a complete materialization. But nevertheless . . . please, into the front room, ladies and gentlemen.

Fat Lady. What struck me especially was the way he flapped his wings, and that one could see him rise.

Grossmann (to Sachatoff). If one were dealing only with hypnosis, one might produce complete epilepsy. The success might prove complete.

Sachatoff. Interesting, but not absolutely convincing. That is all I can say.

All talk together while leaving the stage.

Scene XXI.

LEONID FEDOROVITCH *with the document.* FEDOR IVANITCH *enters.*

Leonid Fedorovitch. Fedor, it was a *séance* — wonderful! It is clear that I must agree to the terms of the peasants.

Fedor Ivanitch. Impossible!

Leonid Fedorovitch. Certainly! (*He shows the document.*) Just think, the document that I gave back to them appears suddenly on the table. I have signed it.

Fedor Ivanitch. How did it come here?

Leonid Fedorovitch. It was here. (*Exit.*)

(FEDOR IVANITCH *follows him.*)

Scene XXII.

TANIA *alone, she creeps from under the sofa and laughs.*

Tania. O thou my soul! Children, children, the fear I endured when he snatched after the thread. (*She squeals.*) But — it succeeded — he has signed.

Scene XXIII.

Tania *and* Gregori.

Gregori. So you have played a hoax on them ?

Tania. What's that to you ?

Gregori. Well, do you think her ladyship will praise you for it ? No, there you make a big mistake; now I've got you. I will tell your tricks if you won't do as I want you to.

Tania. I shall not do as you want, and they cannot do anything against me.

(*The curtain falls.*)

ACT IV.

The stage represents the hall, as in the first act.

SCENE I.

Two footmen in livery, FEDOR IVANITCH *and* GREGORI.

First Footman (with gray whiskers). You are the third to-day. It's lucky the reception days are all in the same neighborhood. Yours was formerly Thursday.

Fedor Ivanitch. It is now changed to Saturday; so that they all come on the same day: Golovkins, Grade of Grabe . . .

Second Footman. It's fine at Tcherbakoff's; when they have a ball, the lackeys also are entertained.

SCENE II.

The Same. The PRINCESS *and her daughter coming downstairs.* BETSY *accompanies them to the door. The* PRINCESS *looks into a little note book, then on her watch, and sits down on the chest.* GREGORI *puts on her overshoes.*

Princess' Daughter. No, you must surely come. If you decline, Dodo also will decline, —and then it won't be anything at all.

Betsy. I don't know. I must certainly go to Shubin's. Then we have rehearsal.

Princess' Daughter. You will still be in time. No, you must indeed come. *Ne nous fais pas faux bond.* Fédja and Koko are also there.

. *Betsy.* *J'en ai par-dessus la tête de votre Coco.*

Princess' Daughter. I expected to find him here. *Ordinairement il est d'une exactitude . . .*

Betsy. He will surely be here yet.

Princess' Daughter. Whenever I see him together with you, I imagine he must have just made his proposal to you, or that he is just about to make it.

Betsy. Yes, I shall probably have to go through that anyway. Very painful!

Princess' Daughter. Poor Koko! He is so enamoured.

Betsy. *Cessez; les gens !*

(*The young princess seats herself on the causeuse and talks in a whisper.* GREGORI *puts on her overshoes.*)

Princess' Daughter. This evening, then.

Betsy. I will see.

Princess. Tell your papa, then, I believe nothing; but I will come to see his new medium. He must only let me know. Farewell, *ma toute belle*. (*Kisses her and leaves with her daughter.*)

(BETSY *goes upstairs.*)

SCENE III.

The two footmen, FEDOR IVANITCH, *and* GREGORI.

Gregori. I don't like to put on old ladies' shoes. They can't bend, can't see beyond their belly, and always step aside; quite different with the young — it is even a pleasure only to hold in one's hand such a pretty foot.

Second Footman. He would like to choose, he!

First Footman. The like of us can't choose much.

Gregori. Why should we not choose, are we cattle? They think we don't understand it; as they were just getting into their talk and looked over to me, suddenly it was: *lay zhou!*

Second Footman. And what does that mean?

Gregori. That means: don't talk, he can understand it. Just so at table; but I understand. You say: there is a difference, — I tell you, no difference at all!

First Footman. A great difference, one must know it.

Gregori.   No difference at all.   To-day I am a lackey, but to-morrow perhaps I can have as good a living as they.   Also lackeys are married, such things have been!   I want to light a cigarette.   (*Exit.*)

Scene IV.

The Same except Gregori.

Second Footman.   That young man puts on a big front.

Fedor Ivanitch.   A vain fellow, unfit for service; he was once in business,— there he was spoilt.   I talked against him, too, but her ladyship was pleased with him,— he outs a fine figure on the carriage.

First Footman.   I wish he were with our duke; he would make things plain to him. O, he just delights in such windbags!   Are you a lackey, be a lackey, do what is your duty; these airs are out of place.

Scene V.

The Same. Petristcheff *comes quickly downstairs and takes out a cigarette.* Koko Klingen *enters, he wears his eyeglasses, and goes towards him.*

Petristcheff (*lost in thought*).   Yes, yes.   My second is "Ka."   Karo.   My whole . . . Yes,

yes. Ah, little Koko-Karo! Where do you come from ?

Klingen. From Tcherbakoff's. You are always full of nonsense. . . .

Petristcheff. O no, listen, a charade. My first is "Ka," my second "Kin," my whole where the foxes say good night to each other.

Klingen. I don't know, I don't know, nor have I time.

Petristcheff. But where else do you want to go ?

Klingen. Where ? To Ivin's, there is to be a rehearsal of the chorus. Then to Shubin's, then to the rehearsal of the charade. You must surely also be there ?

Petristcheff. Certainly, I will surely be there. . . . Up to this time I've acted the wild man, now I'll act the wild man *and* the general.

Klingen. Tell me, how was it at yesterday's *séance* ?

Petristcheff. It was killing ! A peasant was there ; but the best thing was — it all passed off in the dark. Wowó bawled like a baby, the professor kept holding forth, and Maria Vassi-lievna promptly held after. It was killing ! Too bad you were not there.

Klingen. I am afraid, *mon cher.* You know

how to turn everything into a jest, and it always strikes me as if the least thing I say were instantly set down as meaning a formal proposal. *Et ça ne m'arrange pas du tout, du tout. Mais du tout, du tout !*

Petristcheff. Make a proposal to the noble house, that's nothing. Come with me to Wowó. . . .

Klingen. I cannot understand how you can in any way have anything to do with that block-head. He is really too stupid,—a regular stick !

Petristcheff. Well, I love him. I love Wowó; but — with "that strange love," "to him will ever wend his way the wanderer" . . .

(*Exit into* VASSILI LEONIDITCH'S *room.*)

SCENE VI.

The two footmen, FEDOR IVANITCH, KOKO KLINGEN. BETSY *accompanies a lady to the door.* KOKO *salutes significantly.*

Betsy (*shaking his hand in passing; to the lady*). You are not acquainted?

Lady. No.

Betsy. Baron Klingen ! How is it you were not here yesterday ?

Klingen. It was impossible,— I could not find time.

Betsy. Too bad, it was exceedingly interesting. (*She laughs.*) You ought just to have seen the manifestations.

Betsy (*to Klingen*). Come along to mamma.

(BETSY *and* KOKO KLINGEN *go upstairs.*)

SCENE VII.

FEDOR IVANITCH, *the two footmen, and* JACOB (*comes from the buffet holding a tray with tea and a roast; he walks across the room, panting*).

Jacob (*to the footmen*). Your humble servant, your humble servant!

(*The footmen salute him.*)

Jacob (*to Fedor Ivanitch*). If you would only ask Gregori Michailitch to help me. I am tired out getting things ready. (*Exit.*)

SCENE VIII.

The Same except JACOB.

First Footman. There's a willing man for you.

Fedor Ivanitch. A good fellow, but her lady-

ship takes no fancy to him,— he doesn't represent enough, she thinks. And yesterday,
moreover, they slandered him, he is accused of
having let the peasants into the kitchen. If
they only would not discharge him! And the
fellow is good.

Second Footman. What peasants?

Fedor Ivanitch. They came from our village
in Kursk; they want to buy land, it was in the
night, countrymen besides. One is the father
of the kitchen boy. So they were taken into
the kitchen. Just then there was some mind-
reading going on; the gentlemen had hidden
something near by, every one came down, her
ladyship saw them — and the mischief was
done! What, says she, these people may be
infected, and you let them into the kitchen! . . .
She is terribly afraid of this infection.

SCENE IX.

The Same and GREGORI.

Fedor Ivanitch. Go and help Jacob Ivanitch,
Gregori; I'll stay here alone. But he cannot
get through alone.

Gregori. He is awkward, that's why he can't
get through. (*Exit.*)

Scene X.

The Same except Gregori.

First Footman. What new fashion is this now again,—this infection!... Your ladyship too is afraid?

Fedor Ivanitch. As of fire! In this house we have now nothing else to do than to fumigate, scrub, and sprinkle.

First Footman. That's why the air seemed so oppressive to me here. (*Lively.*) It is incredible what sins spring from this infection. It is horrible! As if there were no God! At the house of the sister of our master, the Princess Massoloff, the daughter lay dying. And what happened? Neither father nor mother would enter the room, to say the last farewell. The daughter wept, she bade them be present at the parting,—they came not! The doctor had discovered an infectious disease. And yet there were people in the room with her, her maid and the nurse,—and nothing whatever happened to them ; both are quite well.

SCENE XI.

The Same, VASSILI LEONIDITCH, *and* PETRISTCHEFF
(come through the door, smoking cigarettes).

Petristcheff. Do come along. I only want
to look in at little Koko-Karo's.

Vassili Leoniditch. A dunce, your little
Koko! I tell you I can't bear the fellow. A
vain chap, with the nature of a typical waiter.
Nothing but roving about the whole day long.
Eh?

Petristcheff. Wait then, I just want to say
good bye.

Vassili Leoniditch. Very well. I will go
look after the dogs in the coachmen's room.
The one hound is so furious; the coachman
says he nearly ate him up. Eh?

Petristcheff. Which ate which? The coachman ate the hound?

Vassili Leoniditch. Your eternal . . . (*Exit
taking his cloak.*)

Petristcheff (meditating). . . . Ma-kin-tosh,
Ka-ro-li-na. Yes, correct. (*Exit by the stairs.*)

Scene XII.

The two footmen, Fedor Ivanitch, *and* Jacob (*runs across the stage at the opening and close of the scene*).

Fedor Ivanitch (*to Jacob*).   What's the matter?

Jacob.   They are out of sandwiches!   I had almost said . . . (*Exit.*)

Second Footman.   And besides, our young master was taken ill.   He was at once taken to the hotel with the nurse, and died there, too, without his mother.

First Footman.   How little fear they have of sin!   There is no escaping from God.

Fedor Ivanitch.   So I think too.

(Jacob *runs upstairs with the sandwiches.*)

First Footman.   And then just think, if we had to be afraid of all men, we would have to lock ourselves in within our four walls and stay there as in a prison.

Scene XIII.

The Same and Tania, *then* Jacob.

Tania (*salutes the footman*).   Good day to you!

(*The footmen bow.*)

Tania. Fedor Ivanitch, I should like to speak a word with you.

Fedor Ivanitch. Well, what is it?

Tania. They are here again, Fedor Ivanitch, the peasants . . .

Fedor Ivanitch. Well, what then? I gave the paper to Semion.

Tania. I have given them the paper; and how grateful they are I cannot tell you. Now they only ask that the money may be received.

Fedor Ivanitch. Where are they?

Tania. Here, they are standing at the entrance.

Fedor Ivanitch. Very well, I will announce it.

Tania. But I have still another request to make of you, dear Fedor Ivanitch.

Fedor Ivanitch. What is it?

Tania. You see, Fedor Ivanitch, I do not want to stay here any longer. Ask them for my dismissal.

(JACOB, *rushing in.*)

Fedor Ivanitch (*to Jacob*). What do you want?

Jacob. Another samovar and oranges.

Fedor Ivanitch. Ask the housekeeper.

(*Exit* JACOB, *in a hurry.*)

Fedor Ivanitch. And why?

Tania. Why, you know! My affair stands so now . . .

Jacob (*rushing in*). There are not enough oranges.

Fedor Ivanitch. Serve as many as there are. (*Exit Jacob, in a hurry.*) You have chosen your time badly : you see in what a commotion . . .

Tania. But you know that best yourself, Fedor Ivanitch, the commotion never ends here. There one could wait a long time — you know that best of any — and my affair is for life. . . . Dear Fedor Ivanitch, you have been so good to me, be my real father now ; do find a quarter of an hour to tell it in. Otherwise she will get angry and not give me my book.

Fedor Ivanitch. But what's the hurry?

Tania. But I beg of you, Fedor Ivanitch. The affair is arranged now. . . . I would like to go to my mother and to my godmother first and prepare this thing and that. And immediately after Easter the wedding is to be. Do tell it, dear Fedor Ivanitch !

Fedor Ivanitch. Let me alone now,— this is not the proper place.

Scene XIV.

An old gentleman comes downstairs and silently leaves with the second footman. Exit Tania. Fedor Ivanitch, *first footman, and* Jacob *(coming)*.

Jacob. It is really sad! Now she wants to send me away, Fedor Ivanitch. "You break everything," she says, "neglect Fifka; you also allowed the peasants to come into the kitchen against my orders." And you know best of all that I had no idea of the whole affair. Tatiana says to me: "Take them to the kitchen"; how can I know who gave the order?

Fedor Ivanitch. What, is that what she said?

Jacob. Just this minute she said so. Do speak a word for me, Fedor Ivanitch! As soon as one's wife and children begin to fare a little better, the order comes, go find yourself another place; God knows when I can find one. Please do it, Fedor Ivanitch!

Scene XV.

Fedor Ivanitch, *first footman, and* Her Ladyship *accompany to the door an old countess with false hair and teeth. The first footman wraps the countess in her cloak.*

Her Ladyship. Absolutely, to be sure. I am deeply affected.

Countess. If my health would permit, I should come to see you oftener.

Her Ladyship. I tell you, have Peter Petrovitch; he is a little blunt, but no man understands so well how to quiet one; everything is so simple, so clear with him.

Countess. No, no. I am used to this now.

Her Ladyship. Take care.

Countess. *Merci, mille fois merci.*

Scene XVI.

The Same and GREGORI (*comes running out of the buffet excited and with dishevelled hair.* SEMION *visible in the rear*).

Semion. Don't you run after her now!

Gregori. I'll teach you, rascal — to strike! You'll see, miserable wretch!

Her Ladyship. What does this mean? Do you think you are in a tavern?

Gregori. I cannot stand it with this coarse peasant rowdy.

Her Ladyship (*annoyed*). Are you crazy, don't you see? (*To the countess.*) *Merci, mille fois merci. A mardi!*

(*Exeunt* COUNTESS *and first footman.*)

Scene XVII.

Fedor Ivanitch, Her Ladyship, Gregori, *and* Semion.

Her Ladyship (*to Gregori*). What has happened?

Gregori. Even if I am only a lackey, I have some pride and won't let every peasant touch me.

Her Ladyship. But what has happened, then?

Gregori. Your Semion is putting on airs because he has sat in the same room with your lordships. He feels like striking.

Her Ladyship. What does that mean, what for?

Gregori. God knows.

Her Ladyship (*to Semion*). What in all the world does this mean?

Semion. Why does he always run after her?

Her Ladyship. Well, now, what is it that has happened between you two?

Semion (*smiling*). Well, he is always embracing Tania, the chambermaid, and she does not want that. So I pushed him aside, this way, so . . . very gently with the hand.

Gregori. A nice way to push one aside ; he almost broke my ribs. And my dress-coat he tore! And what does he say? The force came over me, he says, just like yesterday. And with that he chokes me.

Her Ladyship (*to Semion*). How can you dare to fight in my house?

Fedor Ivanitch. Permit me to say one word, Anna Pavlovna. You must know that Semion has an affection for Tania, and now they are engaged. Gregori, however,— I must indeed speak the truth — does not act well, not properly. And Semion, I think, was hurt by that.

Gregori. Not at all ; merely out of rage, because I revealed her tricks.

Her Ladyship. What tricks?

Gregori. At the *séance*. All yesterday's performances were made by Tania, not Semion. I saw with my own eyes how she crept out from under the sofa.

Her Ladyship. What does that mean, crept out from under the sofa?

Gregori. Upon my honor. She also had the paper and threw it on the table. Without her the paper would not have been signed, and the land would not have been sold to the peasants.

Her Ladyship. You saw it yourself?

Gregori.   With my own eyes.   Just have her called, she will not deny it.

Her Ladyship.   Call her!

(Exit GREGORI.)

SCENE XVIII.

The Same except GREGORI. *Noise behind the scene; the voice of the steward: "It won't do; it won't do!" The steward becomes visible; the three peasants crowd past him on to the stage. The second peasant first; the third peasant stumbles, falls, and puts his hand to his nose.*

Steward.   It won't do; away!

Second Peasant.   O, now, there is no harm in it.   We don't want anything bad.   We only want to pay the money.

First Peasant.   Real-ly, now with the personal signature the business is completed, and we only wanted to bring the money and to offer our thanks.

Her Ladyship.   Just wait, just wait with your thanks, it is all a fraud.   The affair is not settled yet.   The sale is not yet completed. Leonid!   Go call Leonid Fedorovitch.

(Exit steward.)

Scene XIX.

The Same and Leonid Fedorovitch *comes; when he sees* Her Ladyship *and the peasants, he tries to withdraw.*

Her Ladyship. No, no, I beg you, come here! I told you that land is not sold on credit, and everybody told you so. But you allow yourself to be cheated like the biggest fool.

Leonid Fedorovitch. How cheated? I don't understand, what fraud are you talking about?

Her Ladyship. You ought to be ashamed of yourself. You have gray hair and allow yourself to be cheated like a schoolboy, and to be led by the nose. You begrudge your son three hundred beggarly roubles when his social position is at stake, and allow yourself to be duped like a silly schoolboy and swindled out of thousands.

Leonid Fedorovitch. I beg you, Annette, compose yourself.   '

First Peasant. We only came, so to speak, to pay the sum . . .

Third Peasant (takes out the money). Finish this up with us, for Christ's sake!

Her Ladyship. Just wait yet, just wait.

SCENE XX.

The Same, GREGORI *and* TANIA.

Her Ladyship (severely to Tania). Were you in the little reception room yesterday evening during the *séance* ?

(TANIA *sighs, looks around for* FEDOR IVANITCH, LEONID FEDOROVITCH, *and* SEMION.)

Gregori. No shuffling can help you here; I saw myself . . .

Her Ladyship. Tell me, were you there? I know everything, confess. Nothing will be done to you. I only want to unmask him (*pointing to Leonid Fedorovitch*), the master here . . . Did you throw the paper on the table ?

Tania. I do not know what I am to say. I only ask whether you can give me my dismissal.

Her Ladyship (to Leonid Fedorovitch). There you see at least that you are being duped.

SCENE XXI.

The Same. BETSY *enters at the beginning of the scene, and remains standing unobserved.*

Tania. My dismissal, Anna Pavlovna!

Her Ladyship. No, my child! You have perhaps done a damage amounting to many thousands. Now land has been sold which ought not to have been sold.

Tania. My dismissal, Anna Pavlovna!

Her Ladyship. No, you must confess. Such tricks must not be played. I will place the affair in the hands of a justice of the peace.

Betsy (coming forward). Dismiss her, mamma. But if you want to sue her, you must sue me also,—for we did everything together yesterday.

Her Ladyship. If you were in it also, surely nothing good could come of it.

Scene XXII.

The Same and the Professor.

Professor. How do you do, Anna Pavlovna? How do you do, gracious Miss? For you, Leonid Fedorovitch, I have brought the report of the thirteenth Spiritualist Congress at Chicago. A grand speech by Smith.

Leonid Fedorovitch. Ah, very interesting!

Her Ladyship. I can tell you something much more interesting. It has come out that you and my husband have been duped by this silly thing here. Betsy says she is to blame; but that's only to hurt me; in reality a silly

thing who can neither read nor write has made
fools of you both, and you believe in it! Your
mediumistic phenomena of yesterday are pure
fiction ; (*pointing to Tania*) this girl here did
everything.

Professor (*taking off his wraps*).   What, that
is to say ?

Her Ladyship.   Yes, that is to say she played
on the guitar in the dark, she struck my husband on the head, she made all your nonsense,
and has just now confessed it.

Professor (*smiling*).   And this is to prove
then ?

Her Ladyship.   That proves that your mediumism is — pure nonsense!   That proves
it !

Professor.   Because this girl intended to deceive, therefore mediumism must be — pure
nonsense, as it pleases you to express yourself?
(*Smiling.*)   Strange logic !   It may indeed be
possible that the girl did intend to deceive, such
things happen now and then ; it is also possible
that she did something — what she did was
neither more nor less than a manifestation of
the mediumistic energy — a manifestation of
the mediumistic energy.   It is even very prob-
able that what this girl did called forth the

manifestation of the mediumistic energy, solicited it, so to speak, gave it a definite form.

Her Ladyship. Another lecture! . . .

Professor (severely). You say, Anna Pavlovna, that this girl, and perhaps also this amiable young lady, did something, but the flashes that we all saw, the fall of the temperature in the one, the rise in the other case, Grossmann's excitement and vibrating motion, how, did the girl do these also? And these are facts, Anna Pavlovna, facts! No, Anna Pavlovna, there are things which must be carefully examined and thoroughly understood before talking about them; far too serious things, far too serious . . .

Leonid Fedorovitch. And the child whom Maria Vassilievna plainly saw. And I saw it also. . . . The girl could not have made that?

Her Ladyship. You imagine yourself to be God knows how clever, and you are — a fool!

Leonid Fedorovitch. I am going; Alexei Vladimirovitch, come to my room with me. (*Exit to his study.*)

Professor (shrugs his shoulders and follows him). Yes, how far behind Europe we still are!

Scene XXIII.

Her Ladyship, *the three peasants*, Fedor Ivanitch, Tania, Betsy, Gregori, Semion, *and* Jacob.

Her Ladyship (*calling after Leonid Fedoro-vitch*).   He allows himself to be cheated like a fool, and does not want to see it.   (*To Jacob.*) What do you want?

Jacob.   For how many do you want me to set the table?

Her Ladyship.   How many? . . . Fedor Ivan-itch, have him deliver the silver to you!   Out with you, immediately!   He is to blame for everything.   This fellow will yet bring me to my grave.   Yesterday he almost let the doggy starve who had done him no harm. That was not enough: yesterday he also sent the pestilential peasants into the kitchen, and now they are here again.   He is to blame for everything.   Out with you, out with you on the spot!   Settle his accounts with him, settle his accounts with him!   (*To Semion.*)   And if you ever allow yourself again to raise a tumult in my house, I'll teach you, you miserable peas-ant!

Second Peasant.   Well, if he is a miserable

peasant, you need not keep him at all, settle with him, and done with it!

Her Ladyship (*while listening to him, she looks closely at the third peasant*). Just look here! This one has an eruption on his nose, an eruption! He is sick! a hotbed of disease!! Did I not say even yesterday that they were not to be let in, and now they are here again. Drive them out!

Fedor Ivanitch. What, shall we not take their money?

Her Ladyship. Their money? Take the money, but they themselves, especially this sick one here, away, away at once! He is leprous from top to toe!

Third Peasant. Entirely unfounded, little mother, as sure as there is a God, entirely unfounded. Just ask, I say, my wife. I leprous? I'm as smooth as glass.

Her Ladyship. And he dares keep on talking! . . . Away, away! Just all to spite me! No, I can't any more, I can't any more. Call Peter Petrovitch. (*Runs out sobbing.*)

(*Exeunt* JACOB *and* GREGORI.)

Scene XXIV.

The Same except Her Ladyship, Jacob, *and* Gregori.

Tania (*to Betsy*).   My dear gracious Miss, what is to become of me now?

Betsy.   Just be calm, be calm.   Ride away with them, I will see to all the rest.   (*Exit.*)

Scene XXV.

Fedor Ivanitch, *the three peasants*, Tania, *and the steward.*

First Peasant.   How is it with the payment now, Sir?

Second Peasant.   Settle up with us.

Third Peasant (*fidgeting with the money*). One ought to have known that; for all my life I would not have undertaken it.   That takes one down more than a malignant fever.

Fedor Ivanitch (*to the steward*).   Take them to my room; that is where the counting machine is.   There I will also receive the money. Go, go.

Steward.   Come, come!

Fedor Ivanitch.   And offer your thanks to Tania!   Without her you could not have gotten the land.

First Peasant. Real-ly, just as she promised she also carried it out.

Third Peasant. She has made human beings of us. What would have become of us otherwise? The land is small, not a hen, I say,— to say nothing of cattle,— has room. Good bye, clever girl! Once in the village, come to me to eat honey.

Second Peasant. Just let me get home; I'll set about the wedding at once and brew beer. Only come soon!

Tania. I'll come, I'll come! (*Squeals.*) Semion, wasn't that nice?

(*Exeunt peasants.*)

Scene XXVI.

Fedor Ivanitch, Tania, *and* Semion.

Fedor Ivanitch.. May God be with you! And now remember, Tania, when you have your own home, I will come to you as a guest. Will you receive me?

Tania. My dear, good Fedor Ivanitch, like my own father I will receive you. (*She embraces and kisses him.*)

(*The curtain falls.*)

THE END.

What's To Be Done?

A NIHILISTIC ROMANCE.

By N. G. TCHERNYCHEWSKY.

WITH A PORTRAIT OF THE AUTHOR.

WRITTEN IN PRISON.

SUPPRESSED BY THE CZAR.

THE AUTHOR OVER TWENTY YEARS AN EXILE IN SIBERIA.

PRESS COMMENTS.

Boston Advertiser.—"To call the book the 'Uncle Tom's Cabin' of Nihilism is scarcely extravagance."

Boston Courier.—"It is perhaps the book which has most powerfully influenced the youth of Russia in their growth into Nihilism."

Providence Star.—"As a revelation of folk life it is invaluable: we have no other Russian pictures that compare with it."

. ## 329 LARGE PAGES.

Price: In cloth, $1.00; in paper, 35 cents.

Sent, postpaid, on receipt of price, by the Publisher,

BENJ. R. TUCKER, · · Box 3366,
BOSTON, MASS.